A KNIGHT SECURITY
SERIES NOVEL
ENTICING
IAN

CAROLE MORTIMER
USA TODAY BEST SELLING
AUTHOR

Peter
As Always

CHAPTER 1

What the fu—!

Ian's shocked gaze remained fixed on one of a dozen security monitors in front of him.

He had to force himself to look away and give his head a shake to clear it before turning back to the screen.

She was still there.

What the hell was *she* doing spending her Friday evening in a place like Utopia, London's hottest and most exclusive nightclub and casino?

He spoke into his hands-free mouthpiece. "Karl, the woman who just came in alone, a brunette, slender, sapphire-colored eyes— Yes, I said sapphire," he repeated impatiently. "It's a shade of blue. She's also average height, wearing a black knee-length dress, low-heeled shoes… Yeah, that's the one. Her name is Eve Bishop. Would you apprehend Miss Bishop and bring her to interview room one, where I'll be waiting?" Ian used the word *interview* loosely. Most times that room was where they took members of the nightclub and casino clientele who were already causing trouble or were about to. "Take over from me here, Viktor," Ian said as he turned to the man sitting beside him. "And turn off the security camera in room one," he added grimly as he stood and strode from the room.

Goddammit, Evie shouldn't be alone in a place like Utopia. She shouldn't be here *at all*. She was a fucking librarian, for Christ's sake, not one of the usual svelte and sophisticated—and predatory—women who frequented this nightclub on the lookout for the next wealthy man who could keep them in the life to which they were, or hoped to become, accustomed.

Ian's steps faltered slightly as he made his way down to the public area of the club, causing him to pause, hand braced against the wall, and draw in several deep breaths.

Evie.

Dear God, Evie was *here…*

"Miss Bishop?"

Evie spun round to face the man who had called her name and was now powering across the crowded bar area toward her. She instantly recognized him as one of the black-suited men standing guard at the entrance of this fashionable nightclub, checking ID if necessary, before letting people in. She had breathed a heavy sigh of relief once she was inside those doors. From the grimness of this man's expression, that relief might have been premature.

Her heart thumped even more wildly, and her fingers tightened about her clutch bag. "Is there a problem?" She used her severest librarian's voice, the one reserved for people who were late bringing a book back and didn't want to pay the overdue fee.

The man, well over six feet tall and built like a tank, just kept coming. "Would you come with me, Miss Bishop." It clearly wasn't a request as he took a firm grasp of her arm and pulled her toward a door marked Private.

Evie tried to break free, but it soon became clear those defined muscles in the man's arms and chest weren't only for decoration. "Would you mind telling me what this is about?" She resisted being pulled through the doorway to the private area of the nightclub and casino. If it became necessary, she wasn't opposed to screaming.

Was it possible someone had recognized her and reported her presence to Gregori Markovic? But how had they even known who she was? She and Adam were twins, yes, but they looked less alike than any normal brother and sister; she was a brunette with blue eyes; Adam was blond with hazel eyes.

But wasn't it a good thing if this man was taking her to Markovic? After all, the only reason she had come here tonight was so that she could talk to the head of the Russian *bratva* and owner of this nightclub.

She relaxed in the man's grasp. "There's really no need for you to hold on to me so tightly, or at all," she assured the man lightly as she stepped through the doorway into the dimly lit hallway. "I'm more than happy to meet and speak with Mr. Markovic."

The man glanced down at her from his superior height as he stopped outside an open door halfway down the carpeted hallway. "I'm not taking you to Mr. Markovic."

Her eyes widened. "Then who—"

"Good evening, Evie."

That voice!

Dear God, it couldn't really be *him*. Not after all this time. And not here and now, of all places.

A glance inside the room showed her it was indeed Ian Knight in all his magnificent, breathtaking glory.

She took in the whole of his appearance in that single glance. At the age of thirty-five, Ian was six feet and four inches of raw, toned muscle. His dark hair was slightly longer than Evie remembered. His eyes were so dark a brown they almost looked black, set in a face that was far too rugged to be called handsome, and yet it mesmerized nonetheless: straight brows over those dark eyes, a long aquiline nose, high cheekbones, chiseled lips, and a square and determined jaw.

He wore an elegantly tailored suit that did absolutely nothing to hide those toned muscles beneath, the wide shoulders, tapered waist, powerful thighs, and long legs.

Evie forced her gaze to return to those dark, narrowed eyes. "Ian." She nodded.

He glanced at the man still standing in the doorway behind her. "Wait outside, please, Karl."

Evie heard the door close and guessed, without needing to look to confirm it, that Karl was now in the hallway on the other side of that door. There was an authoritative edge to Ian's tone not too many people would argue with, even a hulk like Karl.

"What am I doing here, Ian?" The room was bare of all comfort that Evie could see, furnished with only the table against which Ian now leaned, arms folded in front of his massive chest. There were two hard chairs in the room too, one on either side of that bare table. It looked like an interrogation room, which was not in the least reassuring.

Ian continued to watch her through narrowed lids fringed with thick dark lashes. "That's what I was hoping you would tell me."

Now that her initial shock was over, Evie was bombarded with memories of her and this man together three years ago. Followed by the pain of being ejected from Ian's life. Pain that had been crippling at the time, and could still almost bring her to her knees if thoughts of him should pop unannounced and unwanted inside her head. Thank God that didn't happen too often nowadays. Although after tonight, she was sure that was about to change.

Her chin tilted defensively. "And why would I want to tell you anything?"

His mouth twisted. "Perhaps because I'm acting head of security at Utopia."

Her brows rose. "Acting?"

"The other guy is on paternity leave."

"Paternity leave?"

"As in he and his wife have a newborn baby."

Evie wasn't completely ignorant of the Markovic setup, had found out what she could about the man before seeking him out. Which was why she knew Nikolai Volkov, a seriously bad-ass Russian, was head of all Markovic's security and personal bodyguard to the man himself. This was the same man who had now gone on *paternity* leave?

"Nikolai Volkov?" she voiced uncertainly.

"Yes."

"You no longer work for your cousins' security company?"

"I'm on loan from Knight Security."

"Does—"

"Evie, what the fuck are you doing here?" Ian had had

quite enough of Evie answering every question he asked with one of her own.

"I heard they serve great cocktails in the bar?"

She was still doing it!

Having had a minute or so to compose himself before Evie arrived at the interview room, Ian now deliberately let his gaze rove over her slowly, from her head to her feet, and then back again, taking in every single thing about her as he did so. The glossy dark hair, those huge sapphire-blue eyes, tiny nose, full lips, and a slender throat. Her skin was creamy smooth against the black knee-length dress that only hinted at the full breasts, narrow waist, and slender hips beneath. She had a great pair of legs too. Although, like the dress, they would have looked sexier if she'd been wearing four-inch stilettos rather than the two-inch-heeled sandals she had chosen to wear instead.

Evie didn't do sexy. She never had. Which was why Ian had never understood what it was about her that made him want to lay her down on the first convenient flat surface or press her up against the nearest wall and fuck her brains out.

Maybe because, as he had once discovered, beneath that prim exterior Evie presented to the world was a red-hot woman who matched him passion for passion. It had shocked the hell out of him the first time they made love. As had the discovery she was still a virgin at the age of twenty-three. After that night, he had craved her, the feel and taste of her, to the point he couldn't think of anything else but lying between her thighs with his cock buried to the hilt inside her.

That craving for her was still fucking there.

His nostrils and lungs filled with the essence of her. He clenched his hands into fists to stop himself from touching her as that essence took possession of all his senses. Until all he could see was Evie lying naked on her bed, her hair wild against the pillows, eyes dark with arousal, her breasts tipped by hard and tempting nipples, her thighs slightly parted and allowing him to see the moisture slick and inviting on her folds.

Jesus…

Again he asked himself what the *hell* was she doing in a nightclub like Utopia. The fact she'd mentioned Gregori's name a few minutes ago and knew Nikolai was the Russian's head of security indicated she was here to see Markovic.

She certainly wasn't here to sample the exotic cocktails they sold in the bar. "You don't drink alcohol," Ian said knowledgably.

She shrugged narrow shoulders. "A lot changes in three years."

"Not that." He knew her father had been an unrepentant alcoholic when he died, and that it hadn't exactly been a bowl of cherries growing up with a father who more often than not forgot he even had a daughter.

"No," Evie conceded ruefully. "The truth is I wanted to speak with Mr. Markovic."

"Why?"

Her eyes flashed darkly. "None of your damned business."

"Why not just make an appointment?"

Evie frowned. "I can do that?"

He eyed her mockingly. "Well…yeah."

"But I thought… Isn't he…"

"Russian *bratva*?" Ian drawled. "You can say the word out loud, Evie, it isn't going to jump up and bite you on the ass." But *he* might.

Her cheeks blushed at his mockery. "Well, isn't he?"

Ian gave a hard grin. "He's mainly legit nowadays. He has an office in the city to prove it."

"Oh, very funny." Evie eyed him scathingly. "I didn't come here for the purpose of once again becoming the source of your personal amusement— Ian?" She gasped as she suddenly found herself pinned up against the wall by Ian's rock-hard body, his hands flat against that wall either side of her head, his breath a warm caress across her cheeks.

His close proximity was immediate and overwhelming. Evie could smell the heady aroma of his aftershave, heavy with an underlying male musk. Her limbs quaked at the feel of the heat of his body pressing against hers. She felt mesmerized by those dark eyes staring directly into her own. Could almost taste the chiseled lips only inches away. Lips Evie knew could be soft and oh so seductive.

As she had once allowed herself to be seduced.

Not again.

Never ever again.

It had taken her months, years, to get over this man the last time. If she ever had.

Part of her wanted to cry, to scream and shout at him for having once broken her heart. The only thing stopping her was her pride. She wouldn't give Ian the satisfaction of knowing how much he had hurt her when he walked away without so much as a single glance back to see the havoc he had wreaked in her life and heart.

"Get away from me," she instructed coldly, knowing she wouldn't be able to free herself. Her arms were crushed against his chest, and she already knew it would be a waste of her time trying to push him away when his strength and height far outmatched her own.

"What's your business with Gregori Markovic?" Ian took absolutely no notice of her request and remained exactly where he was.

Consequently, so did Evie. "As I said, that's none of

your business."

"Oh, but it is." He bared his teeth in a smile. "As head of security here, I have the final yea or nay in who does or doesn't get in to Utopia."

"*Acting* head of his security," she sniped.

Ian hadn't been at all impressed when his cousin Gabriel assigned him to take over as head of security at this nightclub a week ago. Even less so that it was for the duration of three months, while the usual guy, Nikolai Volkov, took that time off to be with his wife, Daisy, and their new baby daughter. But the Knight family owed Nikolai, and as most of Ian's cousins were off either getting married or already away on their honeymoon or, in Ethan's case, away on another assignment, Ian was the only member of the Knight family available right now to repay that favor.

It should have been one of the other men on Markovic's security team who took over here, of course, but as Nikolai and Daisy had also been personal bodyguards for Gregori and Gaia Markovic and their young son, the three senior men were now assigned to each of them.

Despite his misgivings, Ian had found himself actually liking Gregori. The guys he was working with at Utopia were okay too. In fact, this assignment had been pretty straightforward until tonight.

Until Evie stepped through the front doors and once

again threw his life into turmoil.

He had no idea what it was about this particular woman that merely looking at her gave him an instant hard-on. Apart from those gorgeous eyes, Evie was average in looks, average height, average build, average bloody everything, and yet one look at her and his cock stood at attention shouting *yes, please, pretty please*. A plea that had gone unanswered for far too long.

Ian deliberately ground the hard length of his cock into the softness between her thighs as he leaned forward to speak softly against the curve of her ear. "You stepped back into my world, Evie. Now you'll take the consequences."

Evie felt trapped. Completely surrounded. Not only by Ian's close proximity but also that pervading and seducing musk and the increasing heat of his body pressing into hers.

His more than obvious arousal came as a complete shock to her.

It would also be madness on her part to allow herself to be affected by that arousal. "Get the fuck away from me." Evie glared at him.

Ian's eyes widened at her vehemence. "You don't normally swear."

"Nothing about being around you is *normal*. It never was," she scorned. "Now either get away from me, or—"

"Or what?"

"Or *this*." Evie raised her knee and struck, hard, in exactly the place her self-defense classes had taught her was the most vulnerable part of a man's body. Nature had definitely slipped up there. A man's testicles should be inside his body, where they weren't so defenseless.

"Jesus Christ!" Ian stepped away to double over as the full impact of Evie's knee crushing his balls reverberated through his entire body. Clutching his own balls wasn't exactly a manly thing to do, but he needed to reassure himself they were still there and hadn't been knocked up into his throat, as they felt they might have been. Yep, they were still there, but they hurt like hell. "What the fuck did you do that for?" He gave a pained wince as he straightened.

Evie calmly bent down to pick up the clutch bag she had dropped when he pinned her against the wall before answering him. "Maybe next time, you'll listen when I ask you to step away from me."

"Maybe there won't be a *next time*."

"Promise?"

Ian looked at her searchingly, the stormy blue of her eyes giving lie to her serene expression "When did you get to be such a bitch?"

She snorted. "Possibly after the man I had been dating for almost a month, and who had been sharing my bed for almost the same amount of time, walked out of my life and never looked back!"

Him.

Evie was talking about him.

Ian instantly shut down a return of those memories of the two of them together. As he had done each and every time those memories had tried to invade and destroy him these past three years. "Mr. Markovic has no plans to come to Utopia this evening," he informed her coldly.

"Oh." Her expression reflected her disappointment.

As her eyes revealed her pain of having talked of their past relationship?

If so, she immediately shut down both emotions. "Will he be here tomorrow evening?"

Her determination to see and speak with Gregori was becoming a concern to Ian. Gregori was, as Ian had claimed, mainly a legitimate businessman, and a squeaky-clean one, but he was also head of the Russian *bratva* in London. What the hell could a librarian have to talk to the head of the Russian mafia about?

Ian could think of only one reason. "What did your brother do this time?" Adam Bishop, Evie's twin, had been a fuck-up three years ago, and Ian couldn't think of any reason why that would have changed.

Color first brightened and then faded from Evie's cheeks, leaving them pale and delicate as porcelain, the skin now taut across her high cheekbones. "Perhaps you could tell Mr. Markovic of my visit and my need to talk with him tomorrow evening?"

Evie was coming back here as soon as tomorrow evening?

Yep, her urgency confirmed Adam Bishop had to be involved in this somehow. Ian would make it his business to find out in exactly what way before Evie stepped foot in Utopia again.

He crossed the room and opened the door. "Karl, could you escort Miss Bishop out of the building?"

"I didn't say I was leaving yet," she snapped behind him. "But when I do, I'm perfectly capable of seeing myself out, thank you."

Ian turned slowly. "You're leaving when I say you're leaving."

"You have no right—"

"My territory, my decision."

"You always were an arrogant bast—"

"And, Karl." Ian ignored her to look at the other man as he stood in the open doorway. "Have Ilia drive Miss Bishop home and—"

"I can get a cab—"

"—see that he ensures she has gone inside the building and the outer door has locked behind her before he leaves."

Ian gave Karl Evie's address as if she hadn't tried to interrupt him. Nor did she question how he knew she still lived at the same apartment. Which was just as well, because Ian wouldn't have answered her. He knew she wouldn't have driven here, because having lived in London all her life, she didn't drive. "Good night, Miss Bishop."

Evie guessed from the finality of Ian's tone that not only was this meeting over, but she was being driven home by a man called Ilia whether she liked it or not.

She didn't.

CHAPTER 2

"What are you doing here?" Evie hissed the words at Ian as he stood on the other side of the front desk of the library. She always volunteered to work on a Saturday so that one of her colleagues could have the day off. She had nothing else to do, and she didn't consider being at the library all day to be any hardship.

Ian gave an unconcerned grin. "Fair's fair. You came to my place of work last night. Now I've come to yours."

At least she had tried to look the part when she went to Utopia the previous evening, whereas Ian was wearing a black T-shirt that revealed the bulging muscles in his arms. It also fitted snugly to the equally as toned muscles in his chest and abdomen. Faded black jeans hung low on powerful hips. He wore heavy black boots to complete the bad-boy biker image.

Except, where Ian Knight was concerned, it wasn't only an image.

Maybe he wasn't a biker, but he was a bad boy to his very core.

Merely looking at him set Evie's pulse racing and had her wondering how she could ever have attracted a man who looked like Ian in the first place. Maybe he'd seen seducing her as a challenge? Found the virginal librarian a stark contrast to the beautiful and sophisticated women he usually bedded, and the direct opposite of the air of danger that followed him around like a black cloud?

Whatever Ian's reasons had been for pursuing her three years ago, Evie wasn't stupid enough to fall for his seductive smile a second time. "Why?" Even to her ears, her voice sounded defensive.

"We need to talk."

"What about?"

"You know, Evie, this habit you have of answering my question with one of your own is really starting to piss me off," he growled.

"And that should bother me, why?"

"Because I've only had two hours' sleep."

"Was she worth it?"

He scowled as she continued to ask questions rather than answer his. "You really don't want to piss me off today, Evie."

She ignored his warning. "I believe I demonstrated last night that you should be wary of annoying me too. How are you today, by the way?" She gave a pointed glance toward the front of his jeans.

"Are you offering to kiss it better?"

"Certainly not."

He shrugged. "In that case…I may never be able to reproduce, but I'll live."

"Perhaps it's as well you'll never reproduce." The thought of several small replicas of Ian visited upon an unsuspecting world made Evie wince. "Besides, I thought my questions were pertinent to the conversation," she added briskly.

"At last, a statement instead of a question," he taunted. "And the reason for my lack of sleep is because the club doesn't close until four in the morning, and then I made some inquiries about your brother, Adam."

She frowned. "You've spoken to my brother?"

"No." He sighed. "But I know more about him now than I think you're going to want to know."

Evie looked about them self-consciously before answering him softly. "I really can't talk about this in here."

"And I'm not going anywhere until we have talked about him, so I guess we've reached a stalemate."

"I'll be taking my lunch break in five minutes, if you would care to wait for me outside?" Evie was conscious of the fact that several of her work colleagues were already casting curious glances in their direction. The female ones,

of course; Ian could tempt a seventy-year-old granny into
thoughts of sin.

"I'd prefer to wait in here," he drawled, all while staring
at her with those intense dark eyes.

Devil's eyes, Evie had called them after he'd disappeared
from her life three years ago.

"Wouldn't want you to leave by the back door, now
would I," he added mockingly.

"Go to hell." Evie didn't know whether she was more
annoyed at Ian for thinking she might run out on him,
or that he was right. Until he made that comment, she
had fully intended waiting for him to go outside and then
leaving for lunch by the staff entrance at the back of the
building.

"Been there, done that," he drawled. "Didn't like it
much."

"Your past misdeeds finally caught up with you, did
they?" she taunted.

"Something like that." He nodded before strolling over
to sit on the comfortable couch set to one side of the front
desk.

There was no mistaking the predator he was, even
though he gave every appearance of being relaxed as he
placed the booted ankle of one foot on the knee of his other
leg. After which he folded his arms in front of his muscular

chest and proceeded to watch Evie through narrowed lids.

His casual appearance wasn't as out of place as she'd thought. The library was close to one of the universities, and a lot of the students came in to study during term time. They weren't exactly known for their designer-label clothing either.

Although Evie had a feeling, despite the casualness of his appearance, that Ian's T-shirt and jeans cost more than she earned in a week.

Which wouldn't be all that difficult, she admitted. Being a librarian didn't exactly pay well, but she loved it here. She loved the order and quiet, and being surrounded by the books that had been her escape and salvation when she was growing up with a single-parent drunkard for a father.

She didn't look at Ian again as she continued to work long after the five minutes she'd specified. Linda should have taken over from her by now, but the other woman was well known for returning late from her breaks. For once, Evie didn't mind.

Her thoughts were all over the place as she wondered what Ian did or didn't know about Adam. She had a feeling he had deliberately dangled her brother's name in front of her like the bait it was. Well, she had no intention of rising to that bait. Whatever Ian wanted to say about Adam could wait another few minutes.

Just because she didn't look at him directly didn't mean Evie wasn't completely aware of every move Ian made. The glances he gave at his expensive wristwatch. The muscles flexing in his arms and chest as he picked up one of the books on the table next to him, and then put it down again when he realized it was a popular children's book about wizards and witches. Evie had to hide a smirk at his look of disgust.

She was also aware of the exact moment his patience gave out and he unfolded his body to stand and approach the desk again.

"God, I am *so* sorry I'm late back, Evie." Linda arrived at the desk before Ian reached it, the other woman sounding slightly harassed. "I didn't even have time for lunch. There was a sale on at Benton's, but the queue at the desk waiting to pay was almost out of the shop, and the woman in front of me…" She trailed off to stare at Ian as he now leaned against the desk, a blush coloring her cheeks as she took in everything about him.

The complete opposite of Evie, Linda made no effort to hide the fact she was only doing this job until something better came along. She clearly considered Ian *something better*. Linda was beautiful, and a tall and leggy blonde, so maybe it had.

"Don't do it again," Evie snapped at the other woman, and then instantly regretted it when she saw the amusement in Ian's expression. As if he knew it wasn't Linda's tardiness she was annoyed with but the other woman's drooling reaction to him. Which it was. "You can show me what you bought later." She placed a hand on the other woman's arm in apology for her previous sharpness.

She needn't have bothered, as Linda continued to stare at Ian as if she would happily substitute him for the lunch she'd missed. "Fine," she answered distractedly.

"Shall we go?" Evie prompted Ian abruptly.

He gave her one of those evil grins, apparently enjoying her irritation at Linda's response to him. "There's no hurry. Whenever you're ready will do."

Two could play at that game… "Then I'll go and collect my jacket and bag from the staff room." She hadn't been going to bother with her jacket as it was a warm day outside, but leaving Ian to the predatory mercies of Linda seemed like a fitting retribution for his having come here at all and disrupting her working day.

She deliberately took her time putting on the black jacket that matched her skirt. She considered releasing her hair from the neat bun at her nape, but in the end decided against it. This was the way she always dressed and looked for work. She did give in to a little vanity, though, by adding a coral-colored lip gloss. Not that the mirror reflected back anything other than what she was; a twenty-six-year-old spinster librarian wearing a shapeless black suit, a cream blouse, and flat shoes.

As she had already guessed would be the case, Linda was gushing over Ian and then hanging on his every word when he replied to whatever question she'd asked. Evie almost laughed out loud as Ian looked up and she saw the look of desperation in his eyes. Almost. Because she didn't want to find anything about him amusing. Didn't want to *like* a single thing about him. As he'd said earlier in regard to the hell she'd wished him to, she'd been there and done that, and all she had got for her trouble was a broken heart and a wariness about ever trusting another man again.

Which she hadn't.

Oh, she went out for the occasional dinner or the theatre with Trevor Harris. He was a professor at the nearby university, and a middle-aged widower with three grown up children almost her age. He insisted on calling for her at her apartment before driving them to a restaurant or the theatre, but Evie always said good night to him outside the venue before going home alone in a cab.

Ian Knight had cured her of any romantic feelings she might otherwise have felt for another man. Not only because he had broken her heart, but also because Ian was so forcefully male, and an amazing lover, that Evie was convinced no other man could ever measure up to him.

Maybe Ian wouldn't measure up to her memories of him either. The brain tended to pick and choose what it wanted to remember, usually the good stuff, and— No, Evie might have spent only a few minutes in his company again, last night and again this morning, but it was enough to know Ian was as lethally attractive as he'd ever been. Maybe more so. There was a sharper edge to him than there had been three years ago. As if life hadn't been any kinder to him during that time than it had to her.

Damn it, it couldn't be curiosity she was feeling to know more about those years since she'd last seen Ian?

If she was, it was incredibly stupid on her part.

Men like Ian used and then discarded women by the dozen. As she knew to her cost.

"Can we go now?" He grabbed hold of Evie's arm the moment she arrived at the front desk.

"But I haven't given you my number," Linda protested.

"Gotta go." Ian almost dragged Evie out of the building, only letting her go and drawing in several deep breaths once they were outside in the sunshine. "That woman has the mating instincts of a piranha," he muttered disgustedly. "Or maybe a black widow spider."

"And I thought she was your type," Evie taunted. "You

seemed to return her interest initially."

Because he had wanted to see if he could get a reaction out of Evie. All he'd gotten was a taunting disinterest. "As you're well aware, I like to be eaten *during* sex, not devoured whole after it," he drawled.

The humor instantly disappeared from Evie's expression. "Can we get to the point of why you're here?" she prompted frostily.

Ian had two reasons, not one. Her brother Adam was the first one. The other was the fact Ian had thought of nothing else but Evie since last night. And it had been eating him alive, wondering if he really had reacted as strongly to seeing her again as he thought he had.

He had.

The moment he set eyes on her again today, looking so prim and proper with her hair scraped back and secured at her nape, and her blouse buttoned all the way up to her throat, he had instantly gotten a hard-on and started assessing the desk to see if it would be strong enough to bear the weight of both of them.

Prim.

Proper.

Nothing remarkable to look at, apart from those sapphire-blue eyes.

And yet every time Ian came anywhere near Evie, his

cock stood to aching attention.

A distraction like that could get a man in his line of work killed.

"Ian?" she prompted impatiently.

"Let's go get some lunch—"

"I'm not having lunch with you."

"Why the hell not?"

Because Evie was sure she would choke on it if she attempted to eat anything while in Ian's company. Being with him was disturbing enough, but add her brother, Adam, to the mix, and her stomach instantly gave a sickening lurch.

Adam and Eve.

Her parents had clearly possessed a sense of humor when their twin children were born. Before their mother succumbed to the cancer that was eating her away a bit at a time, after which their father had started to drink and never stopped.

It had been a miserable childhood, and one that had forged an even deeper bond between Adam and Evie than even being twins might have engendered. Their father had died when they were nineteen. Evie and Adam had both been at university, Evie studying English while Adam studied computer science.

As it turned out, sometime during their father's

drunken haze, he must have had a single moment of clarity and had thought to use some of their mother's life insurance money to buy the house they lived in. Selling that house had been their only option if they both wanted to finish their courses at university. As it had ceased being a home years ago, that hadn't been too difficult a decision.

Even so, the years of them both being at university had been hard ones, and there had been very little money left by the time they both graduated. Once Evie finished her course, she was able to get a job in the library, but it wasn't one that paid well. Adam graduated at the same time and landed a better job with a company that designed the graphics for online games.

The problems had begun after a friend invited Adam to a casino six months ago. Utopia, to be exact. The loans Evie's brother asked her for were small to begin with, but had gradually become larger and more frequent. Which was extremely worrying, considering Adam earned about three times as much as she did.

She gave a shake of her head. "This isn't a social visit. We aren't friends."

"And you only *lunch* with friends, is that it?" Ian taunted.

Evie knew by the glitter in his eyes that he had meant the remark as a double entendre. "I don't *lunch* with anyone."

"Why not?"

She could well imagine Ian had lost count of the amount of women he'd been to bed with since the two of them were together. "Again, that is none of your business. Nothing about me is any of your business. So state *your* business, and then get the hell away from me."

His mouth twisted. "I need to talk to you before you think of going back to Utopia this evening. So we can either talk out here in the street, or you can agree to have lunch with me. Your choice."

Which was no choice at all, and Ian knew it. This was the area where she worked, and he had already invaded that tranquility enough for one day. "There's a coffee bar round the corner from here."

"Does it serve food?"

Her brows rose. "Go to coffee bars often, do you?"

"Not if I can avoid it." He confirmed what she had already guessed. "It brings me out in hives when I see people in movies ordering double this in their coffee, a sprinkling of that, a shot of something else. What's wrong with ordinary coffee?"

"I'm surprised at you, Ian." She gave a mocking shake of her head. "Coffee shops are where all the young people go to see and be seen."

"Yeah, well it's been a hell of a long time since I was young. And I stopped giving a fuck what people thought about me long before that. A good old-fashioned bar will do just fine." He took hold of her arm, looking for a break in the traffic before crossing to the pub on the other side of the road. His grip on her arm meant Evie went with him.

"What the hell is this?" Ian muttered disgustedly once the two of them were seated in one of the brightly colored booths inside.

"This is London," Evie answered, their young waitress having already introduced herself before handing them menus and taking their drinks order. "There's no such thing as an 'old-fashioned bar' here anymore."

"Nachos with vegetable chili," he read from the menu. "Pasta with zucchini. Vegetable curry. Broccoli quiche. Veggie burger. Where the hell is the rare steak or a thick, juicy beef burger?"

Evie was having trouble holding back her laughter at Ian's expense. It would be hard to maintain a muscular body like his on vegetables alone. "It's a vegetarian bar."

His eyes narrowed. "You knew that when you let me walk in here."

"Yes." Considering how closely located to the library it was, of course she had known this place had a vegetarian menu. As she also knew Ian liked thick, rare steaks.

Ian looked at her appreciatively. "You've changed in three years, Evie."

"You mean I'm no longer naïve and easily impressed by a handsome man?" she snapped.

Humor briefly lightened his eyes. "So you still think I'm handsome?"

"You were never handsome, Ian," she scorned. "Arrogant and self-assured, with an overabundance of testosterone, but never handsome."

He shrugged. "You once seemed to like me, and my *overabundance of testosterone*, well enough."

Evie had more than liked him. She had fallen in love with him. For all the good it had done her. "And now I see you for exactly what you are."

"Which is?" His voice was silky soft.

Dangerously so, telling Evie she had probably baited him enough for the moment. "Could we get this conversation over and done with? I have to get back to work soon." She placed her own menu on the table unopened. She didn't intend being here long enough to eat.

Ian relaxed against the back of the leather booth as he studied her through narrowed lids, his hands clenching on top of his thighs as he resisted the urge to loosen her hair from that unbecoming bun. Although maybe not, when it had the advantage of revealing the slender and vulnerable curve of her throat.

There was no doubting Evie was putting on a good act, but away from the dimmed lighting in the club last night, Ian was able to see how pale her face was, the anxiety darkening her eyes, and the lines of strain beneath them.

And Ian knew who was responsible for all of it.

Adam bloody Bishop.

He had met Evie's brother once three years ago, knew the little shit had been in one lot of trouble following another after their father died. But this time, Adam had managed to piss off the wrong person. He also, as seemed to be his modus operandi, appeared to have passed the problem off to his sister. Ian would like to wring the little bastard's neck.

He sat forward as he saw Evie's agitation growing the longer he remained silent. "As I said, I've done some checking up since we parted last night. Your brother owes twenty thousand pounds to the Utopia casino."

Evie could literally feel the last of the color draining from her cheeks.

Twenty thousand pounds!

Adam had told her he owed five thousand pounds, not twenty. She might have managed to take a loan out for five thousand pounds, but twenty thousand was a completely unimaginable sum of money when she had nothing to offer the bank as collateral.

"You didn't know how much the debt was," Ian guessed shrewdly.

No, of course Evie hadn't known. She would have tried to put a stop to it if she had known Adam was so addicted to gambling he was risking money he didn't have.

The weakness of obsession was in his nature, of course.

Their father turned to drink.

Adam gambled.

Evie—

She gave a self-conscious glance at the man seated opposite her. *Ian* had been her weakness, his lovemaking her addiction for those few short weeks they had spent together.

But when Ian walked away, it was a weakness Evie had been determined to put out of her life, along with the man who had caused it. Until she saw him again yesterday, she had thought she'd succeeded.

"Where's Adam now?"

Evie's gaze sharpened. "What do you mean?"

"He isn't home, and he hasn't been to work for the past three days."

Adam wasn't at his apartment and he hadn't been to work either? Then where the hell was he? Evie had thought, when Adam didn't answer or return her calls, that he was annoyed with her for not immediately offering to help him, as she usually did. She had never imagined… "How do you know all that?"

Ian shrugged broad shoulders. "I told you, I did some checking up after you left last night. Once I'd found all that I needed to know, I went to Adam's apartment this morning. He wasn't there, so I checked in with the company he works for. There were still some people in the office working, despite it being a Saturday. The guy I spoke to told me Adam hasn't been in to work for the past three days. That he hasn't called in sick either, and no one has seen or heard from him."

"Except maybe your boss?" Evie accused.

Ian narrowed dark eyes. "What the hell is that supposed to mean?"

Evie stood abruptly. "It means I want to speak to Gregori Markovic. I want to speak to him *right now!*"

CHAPTER 3

It took Ian a minute or so to catch up with Evie after she had walked out of the bar. He had to first pay for the drinks they hadn't drunk before he could leave.

She was standing on the edge of the pavement outside, attempting to flag down one of the numerous black cabs driving by, but luckily hadn't been able to find one unoccupied as yet.

Ian's fingers tightened about her arm as she would have moved away from him. "Will you just calm the fuck down?" he bit out impatiently. "Why are you hailing a cab? I thought you were in a hurry to get back to work?" He glanced across the road toward the library.

"I'll call in sick. This is far more important." She renewed her effort to flag down an empty cab. "I'm going to Adam's apartment. I have a key. If he isn't there, I'll make my own phone call to his workplace. If he's at neither place, then I'm going to speak to your boss."

"My cousin Gabriel is my boss, and he's away on his honeymoon right now," Ian dismissed. "Besides which, you don't even know where Gregori is."

"But you do," she accused. "So you can take me there."

"No." Ian felt no hesitation in refusing her. "You're emotional and volatile right now, and you really don't want to accuse Gregori of something he either may not have done or you can't prove he did."

Evie glared. "Are you threatening me?"

He sighed. "No, of course I'm not threatening you. I'm trying to calm you down and make you see reason at the same time."

"And you're failing miserably at both," she dismissed. "Once I've confirmed Adam isn't at home or at work, you can either take me to see Gregori Markovic, or I can track him down on my own."

Ian shook his head. "You wouldn't get past the first bodyguard, let alone the second and third."

Her nostrils flared. "What sort of man has three bodyguards? A Russian thug, that's who." She answered her own question disgustedly. "I swear to you, if Markovic has harmed my brother in any way, then I'll make it my life's ambition to make sure he wishes he had never heard the name Bishop."

Ian gave a slow shake of his head as he stared at Evie, not sure whether to admire her for her tenacity or pity her for her naiveté. "You really do live in your own little fantasy bubble shut away in that library, don't you? Because you don't threaten a man like Markovic and get away with it." His voice had hardened. "Not if you want to carry on breathing."

Evie stared at him, knowing by the steadiness of Ian's gaze that he was perfectly serious in his warning.

All the fight drained out of her, and she felt the sting of tears in her eyes. "If he has Adam, if he's hurt him or—or worse," she choked. "Then I need to know. I have to tell Mr. Markovic I'll find the money Adam owes somehow."

"And exactly how will you do that, Evie?"

"I don't know yet." Her voice rose in her agitation. "But I will get it. I only need a little time. Could you tell him that?" She gave Ian a look of appeal. "Will you speak to Mr. Markovic on my behalf? Tell him I'll get his money for him? Only please, please don't do anything to hurt Adam."

"What the hell!" Ian released her to take a step back. "Could you be any more fucking insulting?"

"What…?"

"I'm employed by a private security company, not the Russian *bratva*. Which means I don't *hurt* people, for Gregori Markovic or anyone else."

"You're working for him right now."

"Only until Volkov comes back," he dismissed. "It certainly isn't in the best interests of Knight Security for me to upset someone as important and powerful as Gregori Markovic."

"You could at least *try*, damn you!" Her eyes glittered angrily, and her hands were clenched at her sides.

Ian didn't like the way this conversation was going *at all*. Evie seemed to be implying that working for Markovic, even temporarily, automatically made him part of that organization. That he was maybe even one of the men who carried out the Russian's dirty work for him. Like offing people who gambled money they didn't have. "Gregori isn't the only one your brother owes money to."

"What?" The color completely drained from her face.

Ian knew how much Evie loved her twin, of the sacrifices she had already made for the ungrateful bastard. But the debts Bishop had now, and to all the wrong people, were way out of her league. She simply didn't have the skill set to deal with this situation.

But I do.

Maybe he did, but he didn't want to get any more involved in this, with Evie, than he already was. He had walked away from her once, for her own good, and he wasn't sure he would be able to do it again if he became any more embroiled in her brother's problems.

Aren't I already involved just by being here with her now?

Maybe he was, but right here and right now, he could

still walk away from her. It wouldn't be easy, and he wouldn't enjoy it, but he could do it if he had to. If he stayed around Evie for too long, he doubted that he would be able to walk away again.

"You're way out of your league, Evie," he mocked. "Gregori aside, you really don't want to go anywhere near any of the other men Adam owes money to." Ian didn't want her going anywhere near those men either. It was the only reason he was here.

Liar.

Ian had to admit to becoming more than a little irritated with the voice that seemed to have taken up residence inside his head since Evie walked into Utopia last night. His conscience, maybe? Whatever it was, it could fuck off back to wherever it came from, because he was not, absolutely was not, going down that road with Evie again.

"Then help me." Evie didn't like having to appeal to Ian for help or sounding so needy, but he was right, she was out of her depth with this situation. "Tell me who these men are and help me to talk to them."

Exactly what had her brother become involved in? And where was Adam now if he wasn't at his apartment and hadn't been going into work either? Could Gregori Markovic, or one of these other men Adam owed money to, have him hidden away somewhere, were maybe even torturing him right now, or already had him kill—

No, she couldn't go there.

It wasn't in any of those men's best interest to kill Adam. That way, they would never get their money back.

Why, oh why had she decided that this was the time to leave Adam to stew on his own for a few days? That he needed to be taught a lesson?

"Stop beating yourself up." Ian sighed his impatience. "Your brother is twenty-six years old, the same as you, and its past time he took responsibility for his own actions."

"By being tortured or beaten up by some of the men he owes money to?"

"If that's what it takes." He nodded. "Adam is a selfish little shit, and you know it."

"How dare you!" she gasped.

"I met him, remember?" he drawled. "He was a whiny brat three years ago, and his behavior now shows he hasn't improved in the interim."

"It was much harder for him to cope after our mother died," she defended.

"And hasn't he been playing on that fact for the past twenty years," Ian muttered in disgust.

Evie's feet were planted firmly on the pavement as she glared at him. "We can't all be macho man Ian Knight, you know."

"Look, luv, are ya gettin' in the cab or ain't cha?"

Color blazed in Evie's cheeks as she realized that while she and Ian had been arguing back and forth, a black cab had actually stopped beside them, the window on the passenger side wound down so that the driver could talk to her. "Yes—"

"No," Ian answered the man as Evie would have opened the back door ready to climb inside. "Thank you."

Evie's eyes glittered with temper as the cab driver instantly drove away. "If you aren't going to help me, then the best thing you can do is to stay out of my way. And find me another cab," she added impatiently.

"I have my car with me."

Her brows rose. "Does that mean you're going to drive me to Adam's?"

Ian was asking himself the same question.

If I drive Evie to her brother's apartment, then it means I'll be sticking around for the duration. And if I do that, I'll also be sharing her bed at some time in the not too distant future. That's a given, because there is no way I can be around Evie for any length of time with this permanent hard-on and not take her to bed.

Saliva flooded Ian's mouth merely thinking of tasting the lush juices between her thighs again. His cock also gave an eager lurch forward at the possibility of being buried in the tight heat of her pussy sometime soon.

"I'm driving you," he confirmed grimly, knowing he was sealing his own fate. For the foreseeable future at least. "I only hope you know what you're getting yourself into."

Evie gave Ian an uncertain glance, sensing there was more behind that statement than appeared on the surface.

Not that she could read anything from Ian's brooding expression once they were seated in his low black sports car and he concentrated his attention on maneuvering the powerful vehicle through the London traffic.

The longer the silence lasted, the more Evie thought back over their previous conversation. She cringed as she recalled some of the things she had said, accused Ian of, in her worry over Adam. There was a possibility, more than a possibility, Ian was annoyed with her for some of her previous remarks. "I apologize."

"What?" he prompted irritably as he gave her a brief glance.

She dipped her head. "I said some things earlier that could have been misconstrued."

"Oh no, I think you made yourself perfectly clear."

Yep, he was pissed. "I needed your help."

"And you thought insulting me was the best way to go about achieving that?"

Seriously pissed. "No," she conceded.

"Good, because helping you find your brother isn't the reason I'm here."

"It isn't?" Evie eyed him warily.

"No," Ian confirmed grimly. "I'm here to make sure *you* don't end up dead for insulting the wrong people. Gregori may be civilized and give you some leeway, but these other men aren't. Also, some of Gregori's men might take exception to you accusing him of anything. They're old-school *bratva*, and no one insults The Markovic without being made an example of."

That may be true, but there was no mistaking the warmth in Ian's voice when he spoke of the Russian. "You like him."

"I like the man I see when he's with his wife and son, yes." Ian nodded. "He also treats his men well."

"It's only his enemies that suffer, huh?"

Ian snorted his impatience. "I told you he's mainly legit nowadays."

"But not completely. How can you even work for a man like that, let alone like him?"

"Who gave you the right to be so judgmental of other people? Of me?" Ian challenged. "And for someone who started out apologizing for insulting me, you're dangerously close to stepping over that line a second time."

There was an underlying warning in his tone Evie

couldn't help but recognize. And take heed of. "I apologize again."

Ian gave a hard grin. "It hurt that time, huh?"

"A little," she admitted. "I don't mean to insult you. I'm worried. Tense. And all I can think of is Adam being tortured or hurt in some way. He's my baby brother, Ian."

"He's two minutes younger than you are, not twenty years," he scorned. "He's also an adult, even if he doesn't behave like one. Damn it, he's the man, he should be the one protecting *you*, not the other way round."

She turned away to hide the tears burning her eyes. "I told you, you don't understand." Adam had the same coloring and similar facial features as their mother, and after she died, their father had been so broken, he couldn't bear to have Adam anywhere near him as a reminder of what he had lost. Evie had become the buffer between the two males in her family, and that protectiveness had continued even after their father died.

Maybe Ian was right, and she should have stopped helping Adam out of the scrapes he managed to get himself into years ago. That was something she could address later. The only thing that mattered now was finding Adam.

She made sure the tears were no longer in evidence before turning back to Ian. "How much money does Adam owe these other men?"

Ian gave a shake of his head. "You really don't want to know."

She winced. "That much?"

"And then some." Ian's investigation into Adam Bishop had been thorough. Very much so. He now knew exactly how much money the other man owed, and to whom, and there was no way Adam Bishop was going to be able to pay any of those men what he owed them. "You do realize there's a possibility your brother has *chosen* to disappear? At least for a while. Until he feels it's safe to return to London."

"Without telling me?" She shook her head. "He wouldn't do that to me."

Ian wished he had the same confidence in Bishop as she did. Unfortunately, that wasn't the case. He had never liked the other man, or the way he took advantage of Evie's love for him, and that opinion had only been confirmed by the things Ian had learned about Adam earlier today.

"Are you satisfied I was telling you the truth now?" he prompted fifteen minutes later as they left Adam Bishop's empty apartment.

Evie was too numb to know what she felt.

Adam wasn't at his apartment, and his neighbors said they hadn't seen him for several days.

Donna, one of the other computer programmers at the company where Adam worked, and someone Evie knew slightly from the calls she occasionally made to her brother's workplace, also confirmed he hadn't been into work for three days.

Ian had told her the complete truth.

Which meant she now had to accept he had also been telling her the truth about the money Adam owed.

She had never really doubted him. Ian wasn't a man who felt the necessity to lie. About anything.

She frowned. "Why did you leave without saying goodbye to me three years ago?"

"What?"

She almost laughed out loud at the hunted look that had appeared in those dark brown eyes. Almost. Because it hadn't been funny at the time, and it wasn't funny now, to wake up one morning and realize the man you had fallen in love with had walked out of your life without saying goodbye or giving an explanation as to why he was going.

Evie had gone over the last twenty-four hours she had spent with Ian over and over again. Dissected every word spoken, every kiss and caress, and in none of it had she found the reason for his having left her life so abruptly.

The not knowing why had almost been worse than the fact he had disappeared out of her life so suddenly and completely.

For days, weeks, Evie had hoped, prayed, that he

had simply been called away on an assignment for Knight Security, one that he couldn't tell her about. But as those weeks became months, and there was still no word from him, she'd had no choice but to accept he had gone because he simply hadn't wanted to be with her anymore. That he hadn't wanted *her*.

Something, after feeling the press of Ian's arousal against her last night as he pinned her to the wall, and seeing the desire that had darkened his eyes to that fathomless black, Evie now knew not to be true either.

And if he thought that by pretending he hadn't heard her the first time, and pride would hold her back from repeating the question, then he really didn't know her at all.

Her chin rose, and she looked him straight in the eye. "I asked why you left three years ago without saying good-bye."

CHAPTER 4

Shit.

Shit, shit, *shit.*

Ian should have known, guessed, when Evie went to Utopia alone last night that she was no longer that soft and willing lover he had known three years ago. He should also have realized this harder, tougher Evie was going to demand answers from him in regard to the abrupt end of their past relationship.

He should have known.

And maybe he had.

He just hadn't expected it to be this soon.

"Well?" she demanded.

Ian frowned his irritation with her determination to get an answer out of him. "Do you really think now is the time or place for this conversation?" They were still standing outside her brother's apartment building.

She arched challenging brows. "I think it's a conversation that's three years overdue, so yes, here and now suits me just fine."

Stubborn bloody woman.

Ian scowled. "Most women would have avoided the subject like the bloody plague."

"I'm glad to say I'm nothing like the other women you've had in your life."

No, she wasn't. She never had been. Ian had known that from the moment he first looked at her.

They should never have met at all, of course. Under normal circumstances, they wouldn't have. Their worlds were too far apart, Evie's in books and academia, Ian having served in the army and then worked as a bodyguard in his cousins' security company the past five years. There was no reason why two such dissimilar people's paths should ever have crossed.

Except Ian had been one of two bodyguards protecting an author who had written a book certain radical factions had taken exception to, and Evie had been one of the people in the London auditorium attending a lecture given by that author.

Panic and screams had ensued when the first shots rang out, Ian and Liam moving quickly to protect and cover the author as the audience all stampeded toward the door. Including the shooter. Once the pandemonium had stopped, there had been one lone woman still seated in the auditorium.

Evie.

She hadn't remained seated for long but had quickly stood and made her way to the front of the auditorium, anxious to know if the author she so admired was unharmed.

Liam had already taken their client to the safety of the back of the building, ready for transportation to his home. The police had arrived on the scene minutes later, of course, and taken statements. Evie's too, as she had chosen to remain behind when everyone else scattered.

Ian had decided, considering it was dark outside and they couldn't be sure the shooter had left the area, that it would be safer for Evie Bishop if she left with them by the back door rather than the front entrance.

He had been lying, to himself as well as her.

The attraction he felt for her had been immediate. Almost like an electric shock arcing in the air that separated them.

An attraction the fevered glitter in Evie's eyes, and the sweet aroma of her arousal, showed she reciprocated.

It was unprecedented. Inexplicable.

Ian was in complete bodyguard mode that evening, tense, alert to danger, and ready to take on any threat, with violence if necessary. The complete opposite of what a woman like Evie should find attractive in a man.

Evie was wearing a gray suit and white blouse, with her hair secured at her nape, giving her the look of a schoolmarm. He had learned later that she'd come to the lecture straight from her job at the library. She was the complete opposite of the women Ian was usually attracted to.

All of those things should have meant the two of them didn't even like each other, let alone feel a fierce and instant desire for each other.

Once the author was safely stashed away in a safe house with Liam that night, Ian had escorted Evie home, and he hadn't left until the following morning. He had been waiting outside the library for her the following night when she left work. And the one after that. In fact, he had spent every night of the next month with Evie at her apartment.

Being with Evie became an addiction for Ian.

Waiting for her every night outside the library, with her looking so prim and proper in one of those suits when she finally emerged, her whole face lighting up in a smile the moment she saw him. The two of them eating dinner together, talking of everything and nothing. Then they would go back to Evie's apartment, barely waiting until they were inside and had closed the door on the world before they were ripping their clothes off and falling on each other like ravenous beasts. On the weekends, they hadn't gotten out of bed at all.

All those things made up Ian's obsession with her.

He couldn't remember a time in his life when anyone had been that pleased to see him.

Or any other woman who had actually listened to him and been interested in what he had to say. Most of them just wanted inside his jeans.

As for the desire... No one looking at Evie would ever guess at the amazing body beneath those unbecoming suits, or the raging passion contained in a woman who looked anything but.

Evie wanted to know why he had left without saying good-bye?

Because if he hadn't walked away when he did, he wouldn't have been able to leave at all.

"It really shouldn't take you this long to come up with an answer, Ian." She mocked his lengthy silence.

Coming up with an answer wasn't the problem. Giving Evie one she would find acceptable was.

Three years ago, Ian had been a jaded and cynical thirty-two years old. He had been shot at by enemy soldiers, terrorists, kidnappers, and even the occasional disgruntled spouse of a couple of the people being protected by Knight Security. He had faced them all without fear.

And yet the tiny woman standing in front of him had

scared the shit out of him.

For no other reason than Evie had managed to worm her way into his emotions.

The moment he realized that, he knew their relationship was over.

He looked at her coldly now. "I didn't want you anymore."

Evie felt those coldly spoken words to the depths of her being. Guessing that was the answer and being told it was were two different things. Besides… "You wanted me last night," she challenged. "When you pushed me up against that wall, I could feel exactly how *much* you wanted me."

"The natural reaction of any man to the feel and perfume of an aroused woman," he dismissed.

Her eyes widened. "I was not aroused."

"Now who's lying?" he taunted. "Why can't you accept it was fun while it lasted, but the attraction had run its course? On my side, at least, it had all become predictable and boring."

Evie felt every hurtful word as if Ian had stuck a knife into her flesh.

He had found their relationship predictable and boring.

Found *her* predictable and boring.

Wasn't that what she had wanted people to think of her, why she had deliberately perfected the art of never drawing attention to herself with her drab clothes and severe hairstyle?

Maybe. But not to Ian. Never to Ian.

Outwardly, she had always done her job to the best of her ability and had never minded working late or covering shifts for other people. She had nothing else in her life anyway, so it hadn't mattered. She attended the occasional academic lecture. Had dinner with Adam when he wasn't too busy.

The only time she'd stepped out of that safe zone had been for the month she'd spent falling in love with Ian Knight.

She'd only had to look at him, with those saturnine dark looks and devil's eyes, to know he was dangerous. An air of danger Evie felt drawn to, like the poor moth to the flame.

She had burned just like that moth too. Inside and outside. Being with Ian had been like being consumed in a hot furnace of desire and passion.

It still was.

"What was it for, Ian?" she challenged bitterly. "Was it a bet between you and your colleague that night at the auditorium? As in, I bet you can't bed the straitlaced virgin."

Ian knew how much he had hurt Evie with his words, could see it in the dark depths of her eyes and the pallor of her cheeks. A pain that gnawed at his insides.

That voice inside him—obviously not his conscience—cried out for him to tell her the truth. To admit to his fears, and why they existed.

But he wouldn't do it.

Because nothing had changed. *He* hadn't changed.

"Don't we have something more important to talk about than the past?" he bit out harshly. "I thought the idea was to try to save that worthless brother of— Don't." He grasped her wrist before her hand could make contact with his cheek. "You should never have asked me the question," he snarled.

"Leave the past where it belongs, you mean?" She was breathing hard.

"Yes!"

"Don't flatter yourself it was ever anything else. I only asked because I wanted to tie up loose ends and close the door on you for good," she sneered. "Now let go of my arm and get out of my way."

His fingers tightened about her wrist. "Tell me where you're going."

"Where do you think I'm going?"

Ian glared his exasperation. Evie had always been stubborn, but this went beyond that. "I told you that you can't just go up to a man like Gregori and accuse him of being responsible for your brother's disappearance."

"Oh, I think I can."

She could, yes. And Gregori was a reasonable man, would no doubt listen to her before throwing her out. Unlike his father before him, who would have had Evie killed for her impertinence without so much as a second thought. Gregori might be less violent than his father, but he was still The Markovic, in control of the *bratva* of London, a title and kingdom he had been challenged for more than once. He couldn't afford to show any sign of weakness, least of all to a troublesome librarian looking for the brother who owed Gregori money.

Ian's fingers tightened about her wrist as he pulled her in close against him. "You'll start doing as you're fucking told, or I'll have no choice but to ensure that you do."

She stilled except for the quick rise and fall of her breasts beneath that buttoned-up blouse. "And how do you intend doing that?" It should have been a challenge; instead, it sounded like an invitation.

"Oh, I think you know how." He lowered his head until his lips nuzzled the side of her throat and he breathed her in. "You were right, Evie. I do want you again." He had never bloody stopped. "Carry on pushing me, and you're going to find yourself a prisoner in a hotel bedroom for the rest of the weekend. Maybe longer."

He couldn't resist the temptation of allowing his lips to caress the length of her throat. Her skin was so silky soft, and she tasted and smelled so good, like sunshine and fresh air, with an underlying heady musk. The perfume of her arousal.

An arousal that was seeping into Ian's veins and clouding his brain of anything but the need he felt to take Evie to bed and keep her there for as long as it took to rid himself of this hunger. Which he already knew he never would. Control it? Oh yes, he had proved these past three years he could do that, even though at times it had felt as if it cost him his sanity. But rid himself of the hunger completely? Never going to happen.

Evie felt weak at the knees from the torment of having Ian's lips against her flesh. She pressed her hand against his chest to keep her balance as the heat of his breath caused delicious shivers to run the length of her spine. Her breasts swelled, the nipples tightening inside her bra. Between her thighs was becoming hot and slick with arousal.

"You can't do this," she groaned even as her throat arched in encouragement to the rough rasp of his tongue.

"Who's to stop me?" He bit gently on the lobe of her ear. "It's Saturday. I'm off duty for the rest of the weekend, and you called the library on the way here and cried off sick for the rest of the day. Your brother isn't around. No one will even know you're missing until Monday at the earliest. Probably longer if they think you're still sick."

He was right, Evie realized. "Don't do this," she groaned achingly. "Can't you see I need to find my brother?"

"I'll find your brother. You'll do as you're told and stay well out of it."

He was really starting to annoy Evie with that "do as your told" stuff. She'd lived on her own since she was nineteen years old, had made the decisions for the family long before that. Her father was incapable most of the time, and Adam wasn't interested. Consequently, she wasn't accustomed to being *told* what to do. By anyone. Least of all the man who had walked out on her three years ago because she was *predictable and boring*. If she gave in to Ian's dictate now, then she would only be confirming that lack of character.

It wasn't easy, but Evie managed to push against Ian's chest and step back. As far as his grip on wrist would allow, at least. "Thank you for your kind offer." She gave him an insincere smile. "But I'm sure I can manage on my own."

"The only thing you'll manage on your own is to annoy the hell out of someone and get yourself killed."

"That's a risk I'll have to take."

It was a risk Ian wasn't willing to *let* her take.

"What are you doing?" Evie protested as Ian bent down

and threw her over his shoulder, carrying her as if she were a sack of potatoes rather than a woman. He pressed the button on his keys to unlock the doors as they approached where he had parked his car earlier. "Ian!" she gasped as he opened the door before lowering her into the passenger seat and strapping her in.

His face was very close to her own. "I'm very angry right now," he said softly. "So you might want to stop being argumentative for the next few minutes, at least."

She licked the dryness of her lips as she saw how dark and dangerous his eyes were. "What happens if I'm not?"

He gave a hard smile. "You've never seen me when I'm really angry."

"I haven't?"

"Irritated. Impatient. Maybe mildly pissed. But angry? No."

The grim tone of Ian's voice and the leashed tension in his body were both enough to warn Evie his mood was balanced on a very fine edge. That it could go either way in the course of a single second. On one side lay safety in her silence. On the other lay a fury so immense, she might never recover from it.

And if I give in to him now, I'll lose my self-respect and every ounce of credibility in his eyes.

She nodded. "I will agree to remain silent. But on one

condition," she added firmly as he would have straightened.

"Which is?"

"You take me back to my apartment, not a hotel."

Evie's apartment, where Ian had spent a month of nights exploring and gorging himself on every inch of this woman's passionate and responsive body, was the last place he wanted to be. But right now, he daren't leave Evie to her own devices, knew exactly what she would do when his back was turned. Either go to Gregori, as she had originally planned, or she would do some investigating of her own, find out who else her brother owed money to, and then go to see one of them. Leaving her on her own right now wasn't an option Ian felt safe taking.

Evie's stubborn expression told him her apartment was the *only* place she would go without putting up a fight.

"Fine." He nodded before closing the passenger door and walking round to the other side to get in behind the wheel and start the engine.

"I—"

"Are you about to break our agreement already?"

Evie flinched away from the unmistakable coldness in the glance Ian gave her. She had only been going to tell him she still lived at the same apartment, but then she remembered he had told the other bodyguard her address last night when he instructed Ilia to drive her home. No doubt, as she was so *predictable and boring*, Ian had merely assumed she still lived there. Which she did. "Could I ask one question?"

"One," Ian confirmed grimly as he accelerated the car into the flow of traffic.

"How long is my silence supposed to last?"

"Considering you annoy the hell out of me every time you speak, until I say otherwise."

Evie frowned. "That seems a little one-sided."

"More than a little," he acknowledged without apology.

Had Ian always been this arrogant and initially Evie had been too bemused by his interest in her, and then totally sexually enthralled, to notice?

Probably, she acknowledged self-disgustedly.

Well, she had noticed it now, and it was irritating the hell out of her. *He* irritated the hell out of her.

That realization was enough to cause her to give a snort of repressed laughter. She had spent the last three years yearning for a man she loved and desired but now wasn't sure she even liked. *Way to go, Evie.*

"Care to share the joke?"

Her answer was another inelegant snort of laughter. Once she started, she couldn't seem to stop. That laughter continued even after the tears had started to stream hotly down her cheeks.

"What the hell?" Ian pulled the car over into a side road and put it in park before turning in his seat to unfasten his own and Evie's seat belt, and then pulling a now-sobbing Evie into his arms. "It's all right," he soothed. "Everything is going to be all—"

"No, it isn't!" She pulled back slightly to begin pummeling his chest with her clenched fists. "My brother is missing. I now know he owes thousands of pounds to unsavory people like Gregori Markovic." She punctuated every second or third word by hitting Ian's chest with those clenched fists. "And to make matters worse, I don't remember you as being such an arrogant bastard. So much so, in fact, I'm not even sure I like you anymore." She began to sob in earnest.

CHAPTER 5

Ian decided to let her cry for a few minutes, but when those tears showed no signs of drying up, he decided to put a stop to it himself. "Well, I'm glad you got all that off your chest. I'm not sure it was necessary to pummel it onto mine but—" He broke off as Evie reared back, her eyes blazing with fury.

"Do not patronize me, you—you *asshole*—mmph." Her words were cut off completely as Ian gave in to the temptation to kiss her into the silence he had demanded and she'd agreed to but so far not given.

Her hands pushed against his chest even at the same time as her lips parted beneath his and she returned the kiss with the fiery passion Ian remembered so well.

He had no idea how or why, but she always tasted of all his favorite things. Strawberries and cream with the sharp taste of a good malt whisky. Or maybe he just thought strawberries and cream and a good malt whisky tasted of Evie?

Didn't matter which. Her unique taste was like a drug

that entered his system and controlled his every thought and action whenever he was with her.

He groaned at the way the softness of her body molded perfectly against his.

And the warmth of her hands against his chest caused his cock to harden in response to having her touch him again.

He pulled her across the console separating them as he deepened the kiss. Her slight form fit easily between his chest and the steering wheel as he continued to ravish the sweetness of her mouth. Her arms moved up about his shoulders as he pulled the pins from her hair. Ian loving the feel of those silky tresses as he entangled his fingers in them to deepen the kiss even more, his tongue searching out and claiming every part of her mouth. Every part of her.

It was the way it had always been with Evie. Pure pleasure. Heated desire. And a welling of happiness inside him so big, it felt as if it couldn't and wouldn't be contained by his rib cage, threatening to burst free. Exposing him.

Opening him up to all sorts of pain.

Opening them both to all sorts of pain.

That realization was like a bucket of ice-cold water being thrown over him, causing Ian to break the kiss and pull back. "I shouldn't have done that."

Evie felt those five words like a hammer blow.

I shouldn't have done that.

Words guaranteed to nullify and take away whatever it was that had preceded it.

Evie had a choice. She could accept that dismissal for what it was, or she could challenge it. "Then why did you? And do not say it was the only way you could think of to stop me crying," she warned before he could speak. "I know you have more intelligence than to think I would believe you."

"Then why do you think I did it?"

"Nor am I about to be tricked into answering the question I asked you." She gave him a reproving look. "That"—she gave a wave of her hand to encompass the fevered kisses and caresses they had shared—"no matter what you might have said before, has been building between the two of us since you arrived at the library earlier."

"You were upset—"

"I said I'm not buying it, Ian."

He drew in a deep breath. "You're a hard woman, Evie Bishop."

"Where you're concerned, yes. I'll admit you threw me earlier, hurt me, with your *boring and predictable* comment. But here we are again, only a short time later, kissing each other as if our next breath depended upon it."

"I never could resist a woman's tears."

"Stop lying to me, Ian!" She snapped her exasperation with him. "I can feel how much you want me." There was no hiding the hard length of his arousal pulsing beneath her thighs.

Evie still had no idea why Ian wanted someone like her. She only knew that he did. They were as different at night and day, and yet the attraction zinged between them every time they met. And it flashed out of control whenever they were alone together. It wasn't the reaction of a man who found her boring or predictable.

"You don't like me anymore, remember?" Ian drawled.

Evie gave him an irritated glance as she climbed back to the passenger side of the car. "I said I wasn't sure whether or not I did, but keep this up, and I'll know for certain!"

Ian added tenacious to the list of Evie's other attributes. It was one he could quite well do without when it came to him.

"Talk to me, Ian," she encouraged softly. "Tell me what it is that makes you deliberately keep people at arm's length."

He closed his eyes briefly and was immediately assailed with painful images flashing behind his lids. Images that still occasionally filled his nightmares but which he could usually manage to keep at bay when he was awake.

He gave a shake of his head as he opened his eyes and banished those images to the back of his mind, where they belonged. "Don't start analyzing me," he derided. "Because if you do, I guarantee you'll find I'm like every other man you meet. We're pretty basic creatures. When we're attracted to a woman, we like to fuck them. When we've had enough, we say good-bye."

"Not always," she reminded him sharply.

He sighed. "Never going to forgive me for that, are you."

"No. And if you were trying to shock me with that comment about fucking, then you didn't succeed."

Ian frowned his displeasure. "I'm not sure I like that word coming out of your mouth."

"Then don't use it to me."

"Fine."

"Now drive me to my apartment, please," she repeated firmly.

"Yes, ma'am."

"And don't try pulling that *don't talk* and *do as your told* crap with me again, because I won't tolerate it."

Ian wondered if it was normal for his cock to get hard—harder—when a woman started ordering him around. Hell if he knew anymore. His cock certainly seemed to like Evie giving him orders, at least. "No, ma'am."

Her eyes narrowed. "Patronizing me isn't allowed either."

"Care to tell me what is?"

"You can drive me home."

"Yes, ma—Evie." Ian decided not to annoy this assertive Evie any further and instead put the car in drive and turned the vehicle around and then back into the flow of traffic.

Which was when his thoughts returned to Evie's earlier statement. She wasn't sure she even *liked* him anymore?

That hurt more than it should have. More than Ian wanted it to.

So what had he thought would happen? That while he was off traveling the world the past three years, acting as bodyguard for politicians, movie and rock stars, and bedding some of them too, that Evie was sitting in England heartbroken over "the one that got away"? Was he really that conceited?

It wasn't a question of being conceited.

Then what was it?

Evie was *his*, damn it. Ian had known that from the moment he saw her still seated in the auditorium three years ago once the bullets stopped. And she was totally wrong about his pursuit of her having been a bet he'd made with Liam: even then, if the other man had said so much as a wrong word about her, Ian would have taken his head off.

He still would.

"You changed the couch."

Evie turned from dropping her shoulder bag onto the coffee table, her eyes wide. "I'm surprised you noticed."

"I liked the old one better. It was wide enough for both of us," he added huskily.

She felt the warmth in her cheeks as she recalled the amount of times she and Ian had made love on that old couch when they hadn't made it as far as the bedroom.

Maybe that was one of the reasons she had decided to get rid of it six months after Ian disappeared from her life. It was an attempt on her part to get rid of those memories of him too.

If that had been the case, then it hadn't worked. Oh, after the first few months, he was no longer the first thing she thought of each morning and the last thing she thought of at night, but she challenged any woman to easily forget Ian once the two of them had been to bed together. Or "fucked," as Ian had put it.

For Evie, it had been so much more than that.

She gave him a bright, insincere smile. "Just as well, then, that your opinion on my couch or anything else is of absolutely no importance to me."

"Ouch." Ian gave an exaggerated wince. "How about I make us a pot of coffee?" He didn't wait for her answer as he walked through to the kitchen area and took the coffee from the fridge and the filter from the cupboard before adding them both to the coffeemaking machine.

His familiarity with where things were kept in her kitchen gave Evie a painful pang, which quickly turned to irritation. Ian had long ago given up the right to this familiarity.

Evie moved to take the tin of coffee out of his hands and return it to the fridge. "I said you could bring me back to my apartment. I didn't say anything about you staying long enough to drink coffee."

Ian leaned back against one of the kitchen units, arms folded in front of his chest as he watched Evie fill the coffee machine with water before switching it on. "The agreement was we would both come to your apartment and not go to a hotel."

"No—"

"Yes. Because you can't be trusted, Evie. As soon as I leave here, I know damn well you'll rush over to Utopia later on tonight and demand to see Gregori. As you intended doing last night before I stopped you."

"I don't need a babysitter."

"What you *need* and what you're getting are two different things."

She tilted her chin in challenge. "Meaning?"

"Meaning I'm spending the weekend here with you. That way I can ensure you stay put."

"You are not staying here for the weekend," she protested.

"Oh, but I am," Ian assured her mildly. "I told you, I'm off duty for the next couple of nights, and I can just as easily make any phone calls I need to make from here as I can my own apartment."

Too late, Evie realized her mistake. She didn't want Ian staying here. Not only did it not leave her free to do the things she needed to do—which was obviously his intention—but it was also too reminiscent of the past. As he had just shown with the easy familiarity with which he moved about her kitchen.

Her lips thinned. "I need to find Adam."

"And I'm going to do that for you." Ian nodded. "But from here. Why don't we both have a coffee, and then, while I'm making my calls, you can go and take one of those bubble baths you find so relaxing?"

The baths she had taken with Ian in the past hadn't relaxed her at all; in fact, the opposite. A bath on her own sounded tempting but... "You're suggesting I take a *bath* when my brother is missing?"

"I've said I'll find him for you. I'll also make us something to eat when I've finished my calls."

"When did you become so domesticated?"

"I've always been able to cook," he defended. "There was just never any call for it in the past."

Because they had always eaten out before coming back here and making dessert out of each other.

"I showered this morning."

"Not the same," Ian dismissed.

No, it wasn't. "Fine, I'll have some coffee and then take a bath," Evie snapped. "But if you find out anything about where Adam is from your phone calls, I want to know about it."

"Yes, ma'a— Sorry." He held his hands up in surrender as she glared at him. "Give me a break, hm? I'm having a hard time adjusting to this new assertive Evie."

"Well, I suggest you get over it, and quickly," she taunted. "Because she's here to stay."

If anything could have possibly made Ian want Evie more than he already did, then it was the flashes of fire and determination he had seen in her today. He had always known she had courage from the fact she hadn't fled in hysteria at the sound of gunfire the night they met. But this was something else. A self-confidence to stand up to him and anyone else who stood in her way. It was incredibly hot. And totally distracting.

Which was something Ian couldn't allow right now.

Evie was right in that Adam had to have disappeared somewhere. It was up to Ian to find out if that disappearance had been voluntary or forced. He also needed to find out those things before Evie decided to take matters into her own hands again. And possibly ended up getting herself in as much trouble as her brother was. As it was, Ian had no intention of leaving her here alone and vulnerable.

He knew the subterranean world Adam had become involved in well enough to know that if the men Adam owed money to couldn't find him, then they would find the next best thing and use it as leverage to make him pay up.

Evie.

Lying back in the perfumed bubble bath, her hair secured at her crown to prevent it from getting wet, wasn't having its usual soothing effect. And it wasn't difficult for Evie to know the reason why it wasn't.

It was the six foot four inches of toned muscle and arrogance in her kitchen right now preparing dinner for both of them from whatever he could find in her fridge and freezer.

This whole thing was starting to feel surreal. The surprise of meeting Ian again last night at Utopia. Having him visit her at the library today. Now being in her apartment, knowing he was just feet away in her kitchen.

She would have given anything three years ago to have had him here again. To be spending the weekend with him.

But all this time later, she had moved on, made a different life for herself. It might not be anywhere near as exciting as being with Ian had been, but it was still her life, and she had forged it inch by painful inch from the ashes of her life after Ian left. He had no right to think she would ever accept him walking back into her life and taking it over again.

Which meant he had to leave, whether he wanted to or not. This was her apartment, and she had the right to say who stayed and who went. She was resolved—

"Not going to happen."

She spun round so sharply to look at Ian as he stood casually leaning against the doorframe that it caused the bath water to swell and almost spill over the side and onto the terracotta tiles.

"Get out," she gasped even as she sank beneath the bubbles to hide her nakedness, embarrassed color blazing in her cheeks as she glared at him.

He stayed exactly where he was. "I've seen it all before." He shrugged. "Right down to the birth mark at the top of—"

"I said get out!" she repeated through gritted teeth.

"—your inner thigh—"

"Get out, get out, *get out*!" She stood up in the bath, no longer caring about her nakedness. As Ian said, he'd seen it all before anyway, and too much had happened in the last two days for Evie to now calmly accept Ian's total invasion of her privacy.

Ian couldn't have moved if he had wanted to—and he didn't—as Evie stepped out of the bath. He was far too distracted by the way the bubbles clung to the tips of her breasts, the slope of her belly, and then down to— Jesus! Her mound was completely bare of the dark curls he had been expecting.

Fuck.

"That's new," he choked.

"Like what you see, do you, Ian?" She placed her hands challengingly on her hips.

Like it? He fucking *loved* it.

Imagining his tongue licking and laving those bare folds and her pussy lips, tasting her cream, made his cock harden painfully inside his jeans.

His mouth went dry as he continued to stare at her bare mound, only to glance up as the bubbles started to slide down her breasts, revealing hard, red nipples. He swallowed before speaking. "Yes."

"Too bad." She grabbed a towel from the warming rail before wrapping it around herself and securing it above her breasts. "I want you to leave. Not just the bathroom, but my apartment."

His eyes narrowed. "I already told you, *not going to happen*, remember?"

"I remember a lot of things, most of all what a selfish, heartless bastard you—" She was interrupted by the sound of the doorbell ringing.

"Ah yes," Ian drawled with a glance out into the hallway. "That's what I came in here to tell you. A guy named Trevor buzzed up to your apartment a few minutes ago. On the assumption he's a friend of yours, I told him to come up and opened the outer door for him."

Trevor?

What on earth—

Oh dear God, with all the turmoil of the past few days, Evie had totally forgotten she and Trevor were supposed to be going out to dinner this evening.

CHAPTER 6

"Where do you think you're going?" Ian reached out to grasp Evie's arm as she would have walked past him.

"To answer the door—"

"Not dressed, or rather *un*dressed, like that you're not."

"Ian—"

"Who's Trevor, Evie?"

"My date for the evening."

His eyes narrowed. "And how long have the two of you been *dating*?"

"How long have I known him, do you mean?"

"Yes."

"Long enough."

Ian's mouth thinned. "Long enough for what?"

"For whatever we want," she came back challengingly as she looked first at his hand gripping her arm before her gaze moved up to his face. "Take your hand off me, and then step out of my way. Now."

"Or?"

"I may have to tickle you." Evie almost laughed out

loud as Ian immediately released her arm and stepped out of the doorway to allow her to pass.

She had known threats of violence wouldn't work on this man, whereas tickling him would. Evie had discovered how ticklish Ian was purely by accident one night when they were in bed together. After that, the mere threat of it had become her last line of defense whenever Ian was being stubborn or annoying.

She gave him a triumphant smile as she walked past him and into the hallway. Her stomach gave a hungry lurch as she was immediately assailed with the heady aroma of what smelled like Bolognese liberally flavored with garlic and tomatoes. Ian obviously could cook.

Her smile faded as the second ring of the doorbell reminded her Trevor was standing outside the door to her apartment while she was salivating about the food cooking.

What was she supposed to say to Trevor? What could she say to him when she was only wearing a bath towel and there was another man in her apartment? And not just any man, but the dangerously attractive Ian Knight. Nor did she and Trevor have the sort of relationship where she greeted him at the door, her nakedness covered only by a towel, with her hair falling down messily from where it was secured at her crown, and her face flushed.

"Having second thoughts?"

Evie looked over her shoulder to where Ian followed closely behind her down the hallway. "I don't suppose it would do any good to ask you to give us some privacy?"

He gave her a mocking smile. "I don't suppose it would, no."

She sighed. "That's what I thought."

"Allow me." Ian stepped around her and opened the apartment door with a flourish.

Evie didn't know who was most surprised.

Trevor, at seeing her standing there in the towel, and obviously not ready to go out this evening. His eyes widened even more as he took in the tall and heavily muscled man standing slightly behind her.

Or Ian, as he looked at the slightly older man with the salt-and-pepper hair and boyish good looks, and wearing an obviously expensively tailored dark suit. She might not have any romantic feelings towards Trevor, but there was no doubting he was a very attractive and eligible man.

"Ian Knight." Ian thrust out his hand to the older man before Evie could make the introductions.

"Trevor Harris." The other man returned the gesture but continued to look at Evie.

Ian took exception to the *way* the other man was looking at Evie. In his mind, *he* was allowed to think she looked sexy as hell right now, but he didn't appreciate having another man thinking the same thing.

Just how close were Evie and the elegant and sophisticated Trevor Harris?

Not so close she hadn't somehow forgotten the two of them had a date this evening!

"Professor Trevor Harris," the other man added distractedly.

Oh great, the man was also an intellectual. Exactly the type of man Evie should go out with, rather than someone like Ian, who had joined the army straight out of school and now worked as an employee at the firm owned by his four cousins. Not that Evie had ever disparaged what he did for a living, but this guy Harris was obviously far more suited to her than Ian was.

Which was a good thing, wasn't it?

Like fucking hell it is!

Harris might be good for Evie on an intellectual level, but he very much doubted the other man could offer her the protection Ian could. Or, he hoped, the physical pleasure.

"Ian was just leaving." Evie gave him a challenging glance.

A challenge Ian had no problem meeting. "No, I really wasn't," he said mildly.

"I'm sure you said you were," she spoke forcefully.

Ian folded his arms across his chest. "Nope. In fact, the

dinner I cooked for us is ready and waiting to be served. Perhaps you would like to join us, Trevor? I can cook enough pasta for three." His narrowed gaze dared the other man to accept the invitation.

"Er... No. Thank you." Harris eyed Ian warily. "I thought we were going out this evening, Evie."

"I—"

"Something else came up," Ian drawled.

Standing here in the hallway breathing in Evie's perfume and knowing she was completely naked beneath that towel, that her *pussy* was completely naked beneath the towel, had ensured Ian's cock remained hard and most definitely *up*.

He reached out and wrapped his hand about Evie's nape, increasing the pressure of that grip in warning as she instinctively tensed in readiness for moving away. "I'm sorry Evie forgot your date and you had a wasted journey, Trevor. But we really should go back inside now, Evie's getting a little cold standing here in the doorway."

"Of course." The older man straightened. "Perhaps you could call me, Evie?" he prompted. "We can...reschedule."

"Trevor—"

"She'll do that." Ian's arm moved fully about Evie's shoulders, and he pulled her in against his side. "Have a good evening," he added lightly to the other man before closing the door in Harris's face.

"You bastard!" Evie immediately moved from under Ian's arm to turn on him.

He scowled. "That's the second time you've called me that in a matter of minutes."

"If the cap fits," she snapped. "Besides, I believe last time I called you a selfish, *heartless* bastard." She breathed deeply in her agitation. "How dare you tell Trevor I had forgotten our date?"

"Did I lie?"

"Well. No." Her gaze shifted from his. "But you deliberately put your arm around me to give Trevor the impression the two of us... Let him think that we... That you and I had been...were—"

"Hey, I'm not the one who answered the door dressed in a towel. Besides," Ian added softly. "It was more in the nature of a premonition than an actual lie."

She eyed him warily. "A premonition?"

"Mm." He suddenly seemed very close in the confines of the hallway. "How long did you say you and the professor have been dating?"

"I didn't." Evie stepped back as Ian took a step forward, unable to go any farther when she found her back pressed against the wall. "Because we aren't exactly dating."

"No?" Ian placed one of his hands on the wall beside

her head as he moved in closer to the heat of her body. "What are the two of you doing, then?"

She frowned her irritation. "None of your damned business!"

"At the moment, you are my business. As is anyone who comes to your door. So who the fuck is *Professor* Trevor Harris?" His voice hardened as he had an image of Evie and the professor being intimate together. Not conducive to soothing his temper.

"He's a lecturer at the university. Mathematics."

"A pillar of the community."

"Yes." Evie sounded defensive.

"Does that mean he says please and thank you when the two of you fuck?"

"Ian!" she gasped.

"Well, does he?"

Evie's instinct was to tell him to go to hell, but the dangerous glitter of Ian's eyes warned her he was once again on the edge of losing control if she gave him the wrong answer. The hallway was also far too narrow for her to be able to get away if that control snapped.

Instead, she answered honestly. "We don't."

"Don't what?"

"Fu— Go to bed together."

"Why not?"

His tenacity was really starting to annoy her. "Ian, I realize that for some perverse reason you find me...desirable. But not every man feels the same way about me. Trevor and I enjoy spending the occasional evening together. We go to dinner, the theatre, or maybe the ballet."

"How nice."

"It is, actually," she defended.

His mouth twisted into a grimace. "There's nothing perverse about my desire for you. Slightly kinky on occasion, maybe," he acknowledged without apology. "But not perverse."

"I didn't mean—"

"I know what you meant, Evie," he said dryly. "Is Harris gay?"

"No, of course not," she spluttered her indignation. "He's a widower with three grown-up children."

"Doesn't mean he isn't gay. A lot of married men are. Or bi, at least."

She sighed her impatience. "I'm pretty sure he isn't gay or bi. Or why you should think that he is."

"Because I believe you when you say he hasn't made a move on you."

"And?"

"And no man who spends enough time in your company could not want to take you to bed. It took me about ten seconds after meeting you," he added ruefully.

Her cheeks warmed. "That's good to hear, but I think you must have been the exception. Now will you please—"

"Oh, I have every intention of *pleasing* you, Evie," he murmured huskily.

Her eyes widened as she saw the intent in his eyes.

"I just wanted to make sure I knew what your relationship with Harris was first. Wouldn't want to step on his toes—or any of his other body parts." His body was suddenly much closer to hers, his breath a warm caress across her bare shoulders.

A reminder to Evie she was completely naked beneath the towel. If she had needed one. Which she didn't. She was as aware of her own vulnerability as she was Ian's increasing sexual tension. "So now you know Trevor and I are friends, and that's all we are. We enjoy each other's company."

"A meeting of like minds."

"Yes," she snapped as she heard the mockery in his tone.

The hand on the wall beside her head moved to her hair, removing the clip and allowing her dark tresses to fall softly about her shoulders and down her back. "We used to have dinner together all the time," Ian murmured distractedly as he twined those curling tendrils around his fingers.

Evie remembered those dinners. Each glance hot with promise. The air between them sizzling with the rapidly rising sexual tension. The same way it was now. The same way it never had with Trevor. Or any other man. "But not the theatre or the ballet."

"You only had to say you liked those things, and we could have gone."

"You never asked."

His eyes narrowed. "That works both ways. For instance, did you know I like superhero movies? Which we also didn't go to. Or that I have a classic collection of superhero comics?"

No, she hadn't known either of those nerdish things about him. "So what are we proving here, Ian?" she challenged. "That we're both geeks in different ways but really didn't know each other at all three years ago?"

"We knew each other in the ways that mattered."

"Did we?" Or had Evie just been fooling herself all these years? Her memories and her emotions clouded by the intensity of sexual desire and pleasure?

"Oh yes," he breathed softly. "I'm going to know you like that again, Evie. Right now, in fact."

Evie moistened her lips with the tip of her tongue. "In the hallway?"

"Yes."

"I thought you said dinner was almost ready."

"I exaggerated. The Bolognese is ready and simmering, but I haven't cooked the pasta yet." He lifted the hair away from the side of her throat before lowering his head, his lips warm against the coolness of her flesh. "You really do need warming up," he murmured, holding her gaze with his as he dropped to his knees on the carpet in front of her.

"Ian?" Her fingers tightened on the towel as he gently tugged on it.

"Evie." He tugged harder, releasing the towel from her grip before allowing it to drop to the floor. "This is so fucking sexy." His fingers lightly touched the bareness of her mound. "It was all I could think about the whole time we were talking to Harris."

Evie drew her breath in sharply, Ian's caressing fingers feeling hot against her much cooler flesh. Hot and sensual and—

Oh God…

Her knees almost buckled as he used both hands to stroke her folds apart. "Ian…"

"Let me."

Let him? She had no will left to stop him. What little strength she had was being used to lean back against the wall to prevent herself from crumpling to the carpet in front of him.

"So fucking sexy," he murmured again. "When did you get this done?" he prompted before Evie felt the moist rasp of his tongue against her throbbing clit.

Her neck arched and her lids fluttered closed as she was immediately assailed with so many sensations she was starting to feel light-headed. "Adam bought me a spa day for Christmas last year," she gasped. "This was part of the package. I liked it, so kept it this way."

"Your *brother* bought you a spa day that included waxing your pussy?"

She gave a choked laugh. "He probably bought it at the last minute and had no idea what was in the package."

"Remind me to thank him when next I see him."

Evie could only gasp and hold on tightly to Ian's shoulders for support as that marauding tongue began to lick her pussy, from her swollen labia to her throbbing clit.

"Fucking delicious," Ian groaned. Her bare pussy was the most erotic thing he had ever seen, her skin feeling as soft as velvet, and her taste was the pure nectar he remembered so well.

"Ian... God, Ian!" she gasped her pleasure as his hands cupped beneath her breasts and he captured her nipples between fingers and thumbs while his tongue now lashed against her erect clit.

It was as if no time at all had passed since the two of

them were together like this, Ian knowing every caress and stroke that would bring Evie to her first climax.

She tasted amazing, both sweet and spicy, her pussy gushing those juices against his tongue, to be lapped up and savored. Her nipples were engorged, Evie groaning with each squeeze and tug on those sensitive tips. Her breasts always had been an intense pleasure zone for her.

Ian could feel Evie's approaching climax as her clit hardened and pulsed against his tongue. But he didn't want this to end too quickly, having no idea if Evie would ever allow this to happen again. Consequently, he wanted to take his time, to feast on her as if she were a banquet and he was a starving man. Which he was. Starving for the feel, the touch, and the taste of Evie.

But not enough to take advantage of her.

"No!" she protested as Ian ceased licking and caressing her. "Why?" she groaned, her eyes fevered as she looked at him.

He sat back on his haunches. "Tell me you want this."

"Can't you feel how much I want it?"

"I need to hear the words."

She gave a choked laugh. "I don't remember you needing them in the past."

"I need them now."

"Why?"

"Because you have to want this as much as I do. The last thing I want is for you to regret this later."

Evie looked down at him searchingly, the darkness of her hair falling forward. "I never regretted a single time we were together in the past. I won't regret it this time either."

That was all Ian needed to hear as he pushed her legs farther apart and slid his hands along her silky thighs, parting the wet folds to reveal the moist lips of her vulva and the swollen clit above. "So pretty." He licked his tongue along those folds until he reached that erect nubbin, pressing and stroking as he slid two fingers inside the tightness of her sheath, seeking out and finding the knot of nerves inside her as he curled his fingers and began to stroke there in the same rhythm as he pressed and stroked her clit.

"Harder," she encouraged huskily, her fingers becoming entangled in his hair as she held him closer. "Oh God, yes. Deeper," she begged as she arched her hips into the thrusting of his fingers, taking them deep inside her as her juices flowed over his fingers. "Ian, I'm going to— That's perfect," she sobbed. "Absolutely perfect."

"Let go, baby. I promise I'll catch you."

Evie believed him. For some reason, she had always trusted Ian with the responses of her body, and she trusted him with them now.

She felt the pleasure rising higher and higher and then

crash over and become completely overwhelming as Ian continued to thrust and claim until she was a quivering, melting mess, her breath caught somewhere between a laugh and a sob.

Ian's arms moved about her when her knees buckled and she began to slide to the floor. "Are you okay?"

A blush heated her cheeks. "That was— I feel a little light-headed."

He chuckled softly. "That probably has nothing to do with my lovemaking and more to the fact you haven't eaten anything today."

It was true the two of them never had gotten around to eating lunch, and the bowl of cereal Evie had eaten for breakfast seemed a long time ago too.

The delicious smell of food wafting from the kitchen area was causing her stomach to churn in protest at that lack of food.

Tension ate up calories. Lovemaking ate up calories. *Arguing* ate up calories, and she and Ian did more of that than they did anything else.

Her legs definitely still felt shaky, and she was also feeling more than a little self-conscious of her nakedness now the euphoria of her climax was starting to fade. She grabbed the towel from the floor and wrapped it around herself. "Don't you want me to…?"

"Want you to what?"

She snorted her exasperation. "I know what you're trying to do, and it isn't going to work, so stop teasing me. You know exactly what I meant."

"I do." He stroked his hand down the warmth of her cheek. "But we have all night."

Evie swallowed. "Ian, we aren't going to spend the night together."

His brow lowered. "I told you I was staying here tonight."

She nodded. "And I heard you. But that new couch you don't like pulls out into a double bed. If you stay, that's where you'll be sleeping."

"Isn't that a little like closing the stable door after the horse has bolted?"

She snorted. "Likening yourself to a stallion now?"

He shook his head. "I'm wondering why the hell I have to sleep on the couch when I know your bed is big enough for two people."

"Because this is my apartment, and if you stay, that's where you'll be sleeping."

He scowled. "You know, this new assertive Evie could get old very quickly."

She chuckled softly at his disgruntled expression. "I'm going to dress while you cook the pasta."

"I'd really rather you were naked." His voice had lowered huskily. "I would enjoy looking at and touching your bare pussy whenever I want."

Her eyes widened, and warmth colored her cheeks. "I am not eating my dinner naked!"

"You've done it before."

She remembered. She also remembered Ian sweeping all the dinner things off the table so they could make love on top of it. "Well, I'm not doing it again now."

"I'll undress too, if it makes you feel more comfortable," he offered throatily.

Less embarrassed maybe, but certainly not more comfortable. Ian fully dressed was disturbing enough. Sitting down to eat dinner with him completely naked precluded her not being able to eat at all. It also meant the two of them sharing a bed tonight would be a given.

"One of us might spill hot Bolognese sauce on ourselves," she teased. "Which would be very uncomfortable and maybe take some explaining if it's bad enough to have a doctor look at it."

He sighed his disappointment. "Okay, go and dress. Dinner will be ready in fifteen minutes. And, Evie," he added as she turned away. "This conversation isn't over."

Evie hadn't for a moment thought that it was.

.

CHAPTER 7

"That was really good," she praised once she had finished eating, the two of them seated—fully dressed—at the dining table in the breakfast area of her kitchen. She had also opened a bottle of red wine for Ian to drink with his meal. Just because she didn't drink alcohol was no reason why Ian shouldn't.

Not that this was a formal dinner by any stretch of the imagination. Evie was now dressed as casually as Ian, in jeans that had probably been washed a few too many times, and an overlarge T-shirt that had once been Adam's.

"Still think I'm a selfish, heartless bastard?" Ian prompted.

She winced. "I was angry with you when I said that."

"But you meant it, didn't you?"

She looked at him searchingly. "And that bothers you?"

"Of course it bothers me." His eyes appeared black, the dark brown iris completely swallowed up by the pupil. "I'm a bastard, maybe, but I'm not selfish or heartless."

She met his gaze. "Tell me you didn't deliberately make love to me in the hallway after Trevor left in order to prove a point?" She saw the truth of that accusation in his eyes. "That's what I thought." She sighed.

"You said there would be no regrets," he reminded her as he sipped his wine.

"I don't regret a thing, Ian. It's your own motivation I'm questioning. Why you felt the need to make that claim at all when I had already assured you Trevor and I were not involved in that way and never have been." It also made complete nonsense of Ian's earlier disparaging comments. "You didn't answer my question as to why you deliberately push people away."

"I believe I was *very close* to you earlier," Ian taunted.

Evie's gaze remained steady on his, although she felt the warmth that colored her cheeks. "I'm not talking about physically, and you know it."

Ian did know it, yes. As he also knew he wasn't going to discuss the reason for that with Evie. Not now. Not ever. "I answered. You just didn't like the answer I gave you."

"Because it was flippant and insincere."

Ian raised mocking brows. "You don't believe I like fucking women? Fucking you?"

"Oh, I'm sure you do. Like fucking women, that is." Her gaze became challenging as he immediately scowled at her use of that word. "But that answer has nothing to do with the question I asked you."

"What the hell do you want, *expect*, from me?" He snapped his impatience. "Will an outpouring of emotional crap satisfy you? Such as I had a terrible childhood? My mother and father didn't understand me? My first girlfriend broke my heart and I've never loved again since? I was bullied and beaten in the army? Is that the sort of rubbish you want to hear?"

"Only if it's the truth."

It wasn't. His mother and father were great people. He hadn't loved his first girlfriend, so she couldn't have broken his heart. He had loved the years he'd spent in the army; most of the friends he had now were from that time. His childhood had been amazing. It had been much, much later when his life fell apart.

He stood up abruptly and took his plate with him as he crossed the kitchen before rinsing the plate and loading it into the dishwasher.

Evie's heart sank as she watched Ian, knowing by his rigidly controlled movements that something he had said to her had hit too close to home. But what?

His parents.

His childhood.

The army.

His first girlfriend.

Something had most definitely disturbed him about their conversation.

"What are you staring at?"

Evie flinched at the aggression in Ian's tone. The wince that followed was guilt laden as she realized she *was* staring at him. But only because she was—

Was what?

Analyzing him, as he had accused her of doing?

"I'm sorry, I was miles away and didn't realize I was staring," she dismissed lightly. "Did you find out anything new from your phone calls earlier?" Changing the subject seemed the best thing right now.

Ian's brow cleared. "Nothing concrete. I have people checking into it."

"What people?" She wasn't sure she liked the idea of these other nameless people, ones she didn't know, being privy to that sort of information about her family.

"My people."

"Who are?"

"You don't need to know that."

"Yes, I do. Adam is my brother, and right now, he's missing."

"And I know how this stuff works, okay?" he reasoned as she continued to frown. "More importantly, I know the people who know how it works. So just leave me to do my thing in my own way, okay?"

"Do I have a choice?" she snapped.

"No."

"That's what I thought." She picked up her own plate and crossed the kitchen to repeat the same process of rinsing and then loading it into the dishwasher before switching the machine on. "Do you want to watch something on TV?" She would have preferred to go to the privacy of her bedroom, but it was far too early to go to bed, and if she did, it might look like an invitation rather than her needing to escape. "I think I might even have a superhero movie somewhere," she added teasingly.

"Why do I get the feeling you're humoring me?" Ian muttered as he followed her through to the sitting room.

"Because I am?" She searched through the movies in her collection until she found the one she was looking for. "The hero in this is pretty hot."

"And that's the reason you bought it?"

And the fact the hero looked a little like Ian. But she wasn't about to tell him that.

"This isn't half-bad." Ian had taken off his boots and stretched full length on the couch while Evie put on the movie.

"Comfortable?" She gave him a pointed glance over her

shoulder.

"It's not as wide as your last couch, but I'm pretty sure it's big enough for two." He scooted over to make room for her as the movie started.

Evie was tempted, but if she lay on the couch with him, they were going to be snuggled up pretty intimately together. Much as she longed to be in Ian's arms again, she didn't think it was a good idea. There was no doubting the sexual attraction between them was still off the charts, but it only masked the tension and didn't resolve the cause of it.

She gave a shake of her head. "I'm fine in the armchair, thanks."

"Please yourself." Ian settled back against the cushions to watch the movie as Evie sat in the chair across the other side of the room.

She instantly felt miserable at his easy acceptance of her refusal. Which was ridiculous when she was the one who had made the decision it was safer if she stayed away from him.

"Do you have any popcorn?"

"Popcorn?" she repeated dubiously.

Ian nodded. "I always eat popcorn when I watch movies."

"Not that I'm aware of." And as she did the food shopping, she was very aware.

"Nachos? Crisps? Chocolate?" He was starting to sound desperate.

She stood up. "I'll go and see what I can find."

She found a packet of nachos and a dip, something she occasionally put out when she had company or Adam joined her for dinner.

Adam.

Merely thinking of her brother, worrying about where he could be and what might be happening to him, caused an overwhelming tide of despair to wash over her and almost brought her to her knees. As it was, she had to lean back against one of the kitchen units and close her eyes to calm what she recognized as a panic attack. She'd had them occasionally as a child but never as an adult.

"Bend over and take deep breaths."

Ian was slightly out of focus when she opened her lids. The kitchen floor was also dipping and swaying.

"Bend." Ian put his hand on her nape to guide her down so that her face almost touched her knees. "Deep breaths." He came down on his haunches beside her. "What brought this on? Was it something I did or said? I know I can be brash at times."

She shook her head. "I was thinking about Adam. I'm just so worried about him."

"You don't always have to be brave or in control." His

voice was as soothing as the hand gently caressing her nape.

Her smile was self-derisive. "I'm very rarely the latter where you're concerned."

Maybe not, but Ian knew she was always brave. On the surface, at least. Because she'd had to be. Mainly because her father had been an alcoholic and her brother always expected someone else—Evie—to dig him out of whatever hole he had dug for himself this time.

It hadn't taken Ian long to realize Evie coped with that responsibility by being the sensible one in the family. The unflappable one. The one who never made waves herself. Always calm. Always in control.

Except with him.

From the beginning, she had given him that control. Trusted him in a way no other woman had, with her body and herself. The more Ian had come to know her, how reserved she was with other people and her emotions, he had realized what a gift that was.

And still he had walked away.

Because he had to, damn it.

He couldn't... He daren't stay. Because the longer he remained, the more chance he had of hurting her and the harder it would have been for him to leave when the time came. As it was, it had almost killed him to let her go. To know he would never see Evie again. Never hold her in his arms. Never make love with her again.

Unbelievably, in the past twenty-four hours, he had done all of those things again.

Oh, Evie had been angry with him at first, furious in fact, but ultimately, it hadn't mattered. The two of them were together again now. And Ian wasn't leaving this time until he knew Evie was absolutely safe.

He kept his hand on her nape as he helped her to straighten up. "Feeling better?"

"A little."

"You really don't have to be brave with me, either," he assured her gently.

Tears suddenly flooded the deep blue of her eyes. "Please don't be nice to me."

"Why not?"

"Because—because if you are, I might fall in love with you again, and I may not survive when you leave a second time."

Jesus.

He swallowed. "You were in love with me?"

Evie almost laughed at the stunned expression on Ian's face. Almost. Because the awe that followed made her heart ache. As if it had never occurred to him she had been in love with him three years ago. Evie wished she hadn't told him now either.

She really had to lighten up this conversation. "You don't have to look so worried." She punched him in the arm. "I was admitting to being in love with you then, not now."

"You never said so."

She raised mocking brows. "Well, of course I didn't. The man is supposed to say it first, and as you were never going to, neither did I." It had been her one saving grace after Ian left, her last shred of pride, that she had never told him how much she loved him. "But don't worry, I soon got over it. Once I accepted you were just like one of those superheroes you tell me you love to watch and read about. Nothing but smoke and mirrors. A myth."

"Thanks." He frowned. "I think."

Evie laughed softly. "Men like you are the reason so many women end up discontented with their life. No mere flesh-and-blood man could ever measure up."

"I'm flesh and blood," he protested.

"But you also save women from being shot in auditoriums. Stop them from confronting the arch villain. *And* rescue them from a night at the opera with Clark Kent."

Ian started to grin. "You don't like the opera?"

She shook her head. "I know I'm *supposed* to like it, but it actually bores me so much, I want to fall asleep."

"And Clark Kent?"

"He bores me too." Saying it out loud made Evie realize it was true.

Trevor was courteous and kind, took her to wonderful restaurants, liked to talk about books and the theatre, and he always kissed her modestly on the cheek at the end of the evening.

Evie felt comfortable in his undemanding company, and she knew he felt the same way about her. She also knew that at some time in the future, Trevor was going to ask her to marry him so that they could continue being comfortable together. He made no secret of the fact he had considered his first wife to have been the love of his life and that he was now looking for companionship, not love or passion.

Until yesterday, Evie had thought she was going to accept his proposal when it came.

Twenty-four hours of Ian Knight, and she knew she could never settle for comfortable when she had experienced such delicious excitement and intense sexual pleasure with him.

She had experienced delicious excitement and intense sexual pleasure. The bulge in Ian's jeans showed he was still sporting a very large and very long erection.

"What are you doing?" Ian eyed her uncertainly as she gave him a gentle push toward the kitchen table. "Evie?" he questioned sharply as she unfastened the button on his jeans. "Don't you want to watch the movie?" Her answer was to give him another push in the chest so that he sat down abruptly on one of the chairs.

Evie laughed softly as she lifted and then removed his T-shirt before sliding gracefully down to her knees in front of him and sliding the zip down on his jeans. "Lift up."

"I don't think—"

"Thinking isn't allowed at the moment." She eyed him sternly. "I'm a woman on a mission, Ian, and you really don't want to mess with me right now."

"I don't?" He lifted up enough for her to be able to slide his jeans and boxers down to midthigh.

"Definitely not." Evie's mouth watered at the sight of his fully aroused cock as it jutted up toward his navel. It was just as thick and long as she remembered, engorged veins running along its length, with pre-cum leaking from the slit at the tip. She heard Ian groan as she reached out to curl her fingers around that silky hot and throbbing flesh. "Still want me to stop?" She stroked her hand down toward the root, holding him there tightly as she ran her tongue across the sensitive tip. She could feel the tremors that shook his body as she lapped up his pre-cum.

"Only a moron would want you to stop now, and I'm not a moron." But he did sound slightly breathless.

Good. Evie wanted him to be as disconcerted and open

to her as she had been to him earlier in the hallway.

She chuckled throatily as she took his length fully into her mouth, hearing Ian's groan as that laugh vibrated along the length of his cock. She slowly raised her head and released him as her other hand cupped gently beneath the tightness of his balls. "Did I do any lasting damage?"

"No," he choked.

"I'll kiss them better anyway." She placed soft kisses against his sac before gently sucking each one into her mouth in turn.

Ian gave an aching groan. "If you carry on doing that, I'm going to come."

"No, you won't." She returned her attention to his straining cock, her circling fingers keeping a firm hold at the base to stop that from happening. "Not until I say so."

"God, Evie." He groaned seconds later, his hands tightening in her hair as he lifted his hips and began to thrust into her mouth. "I need— Let me— You're killing me!" he gasped as she ignored him and continued the remorseless torment. "Don't stop!" he cried out seconds later as she released him from her mouth with a loud pop.

Evie licked his pre-cum from her slightly swollen lips as she looked at him from beneath lowered lashes. "I'm in no hurry. Are you?"

"No, but— Jesus. It's been too fucking long to play

games with me."

"I'm not playing games," she assured him.

He sat forward in the chair to grasp the tops of her arms. "Neither can you go all aggressive on me like that, take me to the edge, and then fucking stop!" His eyes were dark and wild.

She gave a slow and wicked smile. "I thought I just did."

Ian's breath caught in his throat as her fingers tightened about his cock once more and began a slow and tortuous stroke along its quivering length, her fingers swirling over the sensitive tip before repeating the movement. Her other hand moved to his bare chest, the tips of her fingers tracing a light and sensuous pattern from one pebbled nipple to the other. It was a barely there touch, but the dual assault was enough to cause his body to tremble and quake and his nipples to tighten in painful arousal.

"Take off your top and bra and let me see your breasts when I come," he instructed softly.

She gave him a sideways glance. "Didn't you forget something?"

"Please," he bit out between clenched teeth.

Her smile was pure seductress as she rose back to her feet and peeled off the overlarge T-shirt. The bra followed, allowing her breasts to tumble free of the lace cups as she slid the straps down her arms before discarding it completely.

Ian pulled her gently forward to stand between his parted thighs, his arms going about her waist as he nuzzled his face against the dip between her breasts. "I love having your mouth on me, but I've missed this too." When they were together before, he had woken on so many mornings with his head resting on the soft pillow of her breasts.

"You knew where I was," she said huskily, her fingers threading lightly in his hair.

He had always known. He might not have seen Evie for three years, but that didn't mean he hadn't hired someone to reassure him on a regular basis that she was well, still living in the same apartment and working at the library.

Some people might consider that interest stalkerish, but Ian had made sure Evie never knew about it. Nor did he attempt to see her again. It was enough for him to know she was safe and continuing with her life.

None of those reports had told him about Trevor Harris. Nor had Ian had any idea how jealous he would feel about there being another man in her life until Harris buzzed up to her apartment earlier.

He had wanted to kill the guy and bury the body where no one would ever find it.

Oh, very civilized, Ian.

That wasn't a word that ever came to mind when he thought of Evie. Primitive, wild, maybe even caveman, but never civilized.

It was also dog-in-the-manger of him. Evie was only twenty-six years old, and one day she was going to want to be married and have children of her own. Ian thought he had accepted long ago that Evie's husband and the father of her children wasn't going to be him.

Dismissing someone who didn't exist yet had been easy. Tonight he had been face-to-face with the possible reality of that man. Only Evie's presence had stopped that meeting from becoming a bloody one.

Evie leaned back to look at him. "Are you okay?"

It was the first indication Ian had that he had actually groaned out loud at that realization. "I'm fine." He nodded abruptly. "Are you going to finish this, or shall I just chalk it up to you having become a major cock tease?"

Evie drew her breath in sharply, her troubled gaze searching the hard lines of Ian's face. His eyes were once again those glittering dark devil's eyes. "I think you may have just killed the mood."

"I think it had already died." He stood up to move away and straighten and refasten his clothing. "I'm going to watch the end of the movie." He strode off without looking at her again, and the volume on the TV turned up seconds later.

Leaving a half-naked—and humiliated—Evie kneeling on the floor.

CHAPTER 8

"If that's your boyfriend again, I may not be as polite as I was last night."

Evie felt totally disorientated, both by the hot, naked body curled intimately behind and against hers in the bed, the bare arm thrown about her waist, and the buzz of the intercom for the outer door of the apartment building.

She didn't know which to answer first.

For one thing, Ian certainly hadn't been in bed with her when she fell asleep last night. In fact, he hadn't even glanced her way but continued to watch the movie, after muttering "'Night" in response to her announcement she was going to bed and there were clean sheets and blankets in the cupboard in the hallway.

Nor did she normally receive visitors on a Sunday at the uncivilized time of seven thirty in the morning the digital clock on top of her bedside cabinet said it was. Unless—

"Maybe it's Adam?" Ian suggested sleepily.

That had been Evie's own thought.

Until she remembered that Adam had his own key. They had keys to each other's apartment.

"Are you going to answer that, or shall I?" Ian prompted as the buzzer sounded a second time.

"I am." Evie threw back the bedclothes before scooting over to the side of the bed and standing. "You might want to put some clothes on while I'm gone," she advised. "And maybe come up with an explanation as to what you're doing in my bed." She left the bedroom without having looked at him.

Looking at Ian first thing in the morning was just too much after their disagreement last night. Besides, she already knew how he would look. Dark hair tousled. Dark eyes drowsily sexy. His cock hard and ready for morning sex.

She'd been there, done that. Had the T-shirt and the commemorative mug to prove it.

Making love to him last night had been a mistake. She wasn't about to make it worse by repeating the experience this morning.

Ian watched beneath lowered lids as Evie left the bedroom before getting himself out of bed. He pulled on and zipped his jeans before following her. If this was Harris, having thought about the situation overnight and come back this morning to demand an explanation for Ian's presence in Evie's apartment last night, then Ian wanted the other man to know he was still here.

He found Evie making coffee in the kitchen area in the nightshirt he had discovered she was wearing in bed last night when he crawled beneath the bedcovers next to her.

She glanced at him before taking a third mug from the overhead cupboard, the nightshirt riding up the bareness of her thighs as she raised her arm. "I've folded and put away the sheets and blankets from the sitting room, and your friend Nikolai is on his way up."

Ian came to an abrupt halt on the other side of the breakfast bar. "Volkov?"

She raised mocking brows. "Do you know another Nikolai?"

No, he didn't. But he didn't know this one well enough either for the other man to be paying him early morning visits. How the hell had Nikolai even known to find him here in the first place?

Evie turned to lean back against the kitchen unit as the coffee started to percolate, filling the kitchen with its ambrosial smell. "I don't appreciate you telling a man like Nikolai Volkov where I live."

Ian frowned at the accusation in her tone. Last night, things had quickly gone to hell between the two of them, and he accepted he was to blame for most of that. But he wasn't about to accept responsibility for something he didn't do. "I—" He broke off as the doorbell rang. "For the record, I'm not responsible for Nikolai being here. The man is a fucking law unto himself. And for God's sake, go and put some clothes on while I answer the door," he snarled.

She raised taunting brows. "For *whose* sake?"

"Just do it, Evie," he snapped before marching down the hallway.

Evie didn't move. She couldn't move, her legs seeming to be locked in place. And not just because the powerful Nikolai Volkov would very shortly be inside her apartment.

Ian's hair had been as tousled as she had known it would be. There was also a morning shadow darkening his jaw. But his eyes were hard and glittering rather than warm and inviting. He also appeared to be wearing only his jeans, the zip fastened but the top button left undone, and giving her a tantalizing and mouthwatering glimpse of the top of his engorged and only-just confined cock.

The only thing that finally allowed her to move was that she really didn't want to still be in her nightgown when she met Nikolai Volkov for the first time.

Ian fastened the top button on his jeans before wrenching the apartment door open to glare at the other man. "What could you possibly want at seven thirty on a Sunday morning, Nikolai?"

Nikolai's eyes narrowed at Ian's aggression. The

Russian was only an inch or so shorter than Ian, his frame as muscular. His stillness, as he continued to look at Ian with icy-gray eyes—killer's eyes?—was as unnerving as the predatory grace with which he moved. Ian had only ever seen the Russian in one of the expensively tailored dark suits he favored before today, but the other man appeared no less intimidating in a fitted black T-shirt, black jeans, and heavy black boots.

Ian deliberately placed one of his hands on the doorframe and the other on the door, his message very clear as he filled the space in between. Nikolai wasn't getting inside until he had stated his reason for being here.

"I advise that you moderate your tone when talking to me, Knight," the Russian warned softly. "You were the one who came to me for help, remember."

Of course Ian remembered. Nikolai had been one of several phone calls he had made the previous evening while Evie was taking a bath. "Do you have some information for me?"

Those gray eyes became glacial. "I have some information for Miss Bishop."

"Anything you have to say to Evie—"

"You can come in and say to me," Evie spoke from behind him. "Please come in, Mr. Volkov. I've just made some fresh coffee. Ian," she prompted sharply as he still blocked the doorway.

Ian gave the other man a warning glance as he stepped aside and allowed him entry.

"Mr. Knight and I will join you very shortly, Miss Bishop," Nikolai said evenly once he was inside the apartment.

Ian winced as he saw the angry flush in Evie's cheeks at the other man's dismissal in her own apartment. Justified, perhaps, but Nikolai was not the man for her to lose her temper with.

"I'll go and pour the coffee." Thankfully, she wisely only shot Ian a baleful glare—what the hell did he do?— before stomping back off to the kitchen.

Nikolai's expression lightened fractionally as he took in Ian's bare-chested appearance. "Did I interrupt something?"

"Not quite," Ian rasped. "But I had high hopes."

The other man nodded. "I had no idea Adam Bishop's sister was so beautiful."

Ian just as wisely didn't rise to what he was sure was a comment meant to deliberately annoy him. Nikolai was totally in love with and devoted to his wife, Daisy. "You *know* Adam?"

The Russian's top lip turned back with distaste. "Unfortunately, I have had reason to…speak with him on occasion at Utopia, yes." He glanced toward the kitchen.

"From the little I have seen of Miss Bishop, it would seem that of the two, she was the one to receive all the balls when they were together in the womb."

Ian didn't remember ever telling the other man that Evie and Adam were twins. Which meant, despite being on paternity leave, Nikolai had been doing some investigating of his own since Ian's phone call the previous day. "I hope you aren't here to tell her something has happened to her brother."

The Russian arched blond brows. "As I only intend to have this conversation once, I suggest we join Miss Bishop in the kitchen."

Ian placed a hand on Nikolai's arm, refusing to remove it when the other man glanced pointedly down at that hand. "Just tell me Bishop is still alive." Ian might think Adam was a little shit, but it would break Evie's heart if anything were to happen to her brother.

Nikolai nodded abruptly. "He is still alive."

Ian released the breath he hadn't realized he'd been holding. He also removed his hand from Nikolai's arm. "Let's go and have that coffee before Evie comes looking for us and we both feel the sharp edge of her tongue."

Nikolai gave a wolfish grin. "She has you pussy-whipped already, my friend."

Ian's grimace was self-derisive. "Never think it to look

at her, would you."

"I have learned it is the quiet ones we should be most wary of." Nikolai's tone was affectionate as he obviously referred to his wife.

Ian was far from pleased when the two men entered the kitchen area and he saw exactly what Evie was wearing and immediately reversed his previous opinion of her. She *did* do sexy, after all.

The jeans she was wearing today fit snugly to her hips and legs. The pink vest-top was also figure-hugging and emphasized the curve of her breasts. He scowled his displeasure.

Evie had no idea what the two men had talked about during the few minutes they had remained in the hallway, but the tension had obviously lessened between them by the time they joined her in the kitchen. The focus of Ian's scowl now seemed to be directed at her.

Nikolai Volkov was as scary as she had imagined he would be. He possessed a predatory stillness that matched the wolf his surname translated to. She also had no doubt his pale gray eyes could turn to ice when he was displeased. But there were also laughter lines beside those cool gray eyes and grooved into the hardness of his cheeks.

"Ian tells me you and your wife recently had a daughter, Mr. Volkov?" she prompted politely as she ignored

Ian's glowering demeanor to hand the Russian a mug of strong coffee, putting cream and sugar on the breakfast bar for him to help himself. She poured coffee into two more mugs and placed one of them on the breakfast bar for Ian.

"Natasha." The Russian's expression instantly softened. "She is a month old and the reason for the early hour of my visit. Tasha has her days and nights confused at the moment, and last night it was my turn to stay up with her while my wife slept. Daisy is now awake and rested and has taken over." He ignored the cream and sugar, as did Ian, both men sipping the black coffee with obvious relish.

Even so, Evie sensed the restlessness coming off Ian in hostile waves as he watched the other man through narrowed lids. Unfortunately, Volkov also sensed that impatience, and he was obviously enjoying himself at Ian's expense.

"Why don't you go and put the rest of your clothes on?" She was finding a bare-chested Ian totally unnerving.

"I'm fine as I am, thanks," he bit out tersely.

"So, Miss Bishop." The Russian turned to her and ignored the glowering Ian. "It would seem that your brother is currently working for the Romanian mafia. Cezar Fescaru, to be exact."

"What?" Evie felt her face pale as she reached out blindly to grasp the edge of the breakfast bar for support.

Volkov nodded. "Your brother is an expert at computer hacking, is he not?"

"He works as a troubleshooter for an online gaming company," she defended.

The Russian's expression softened slightly. "He is now using that ability to aid the Fescaru family with their lucrative online scamming business."

Adam had always been amazing with numbers, and that gift had served him very well when he took a degree in computer science. But what Nikolai Volkov was suggesting was way out of the realm of writing and implementing the computer software for the online games specialized in by the company Adam worked for.

She gave a shake of her head. "I think you have him confused with someone else. Adam isn't always sensible, but he would never do anything illegal."

Evie made the statement firmly enough, but was she absolutely sure about that?

Much as Evie loved her brother, she hadn't thought him capable of putting himself thousands of pounds in debt to the Russian mafia either. Was it so far a stretch to accept he might be doing something illegal to get himself out of that debt?

The scathing expression now on Ian's face said he could easily believe Adam capable of doing exactly that.

"Fescaru must be forcing Adam to work for him," she insisted stubbornly.

The Russian gave a shrug of his wide shoulders. "My information says he is…giving his assistance in exchange for the money they loaned him and he is unable to pay back."

Which, Evie guessed, was Nikolai's polite way of saying Adam wasn't being coerced.

Adam asking for Evie's help had obviously been the very last resort, and the first time, she had refused to help him pay off his debts. To teach him a lesson. Hah. The only lesson Adam seemed to have learned was how to work for the Romanian mafia.

"Where is he now?" she asked.

"I believe Cezar Fescaru operates from a warehouse a mile or so from Canary Wharf."

"You believe, or you know?"

Ian winced at Evie's accusing tone. Nikolai might be being polite at the moment, but Ian doubted he would continue to be so if Evie continued to talk to him in this aggressive way. "Evie—"

"It is my business to know," Volkov confirmed over Ian's warning, his pale gaze narrowed on Evie. "The Fescaru family only recently moved some of their scamming operation to London. As it does not interfere with Markovic business, it has been allowed."

"What happens when it ceases not to interfere with the Markovic business?" Evie scorned.

"I think it's time we thanked Nikolai for his time and the information and allowed him to return to his wife and daughter," Ian put in firmly.

"But—"

"Evie, quit while you're ahead, hmm?" he advised harshly.

She scowled at him. "I need Mr. Volkov to give us a more precise location so I can go and talk to Cezar Fescaru and have him release Adam."

"You aren't going anywhere near the Fescaru family." The violence Ian had heard connected to the Romanian mafia since they moved to London made every other mafia family, of whatever nationality, look like a load of pussies. Adam was of use to them right now, but the Romanians wouldn't hesitate to eliminate Evie if she became a problem. Ian's hands clenched at his sides with the need he felt to put them around Adam Bishop's throat for having involved his sister in this dangerous situation.

"I don't think it's your decision where I do or don't go," Evie answered tartly.

His mouth thinned. "I'm making it so." The Romanians would eat Evie up and spit her out again without a second thought.

"Well, you can just *un*make it." She glared. "Because I'll do whatever I have to do to get Adam free of their clutches."

Ian could feel a nerve pulsing in his clenched jaw. "You won't succeed in doing that by rushing over there completely unprepared and without backup."

"You can be my backup if you feel so strongly about it," she challenged.

He frowned his frustration. "So you can get us both killed?"

"I have no intention of anyone being killed. I just want my brother released," she maintained stubbornly. "And if you won't come with me, I'll go on my own."

"Nikolai, a little help here, please," Ian appealed to the other man.

The Russian smirked. "I made the necessary inquiries and have told you what you wanted to know. It is now up to you to keep your own woman in check—"

"I'm not *his woman*!" Evie was red-faced with outrage.

"In this situation, that's exactly what you are, and don't ever think otherwise," Ian snapped. "And I say you aren't going anywhere near Cezar Fescaru."

Her eyes glittered with temper. "I'll do what I damn well please, and *you* can take your macho-man crap and stick it where the sun don't shine!"

"We'll continue this discussion after Nikolai leaves," Ian

stated icily. "Thank you for taking the time and trouble to come here personally to inform us where Adam is, Nikolai. I appreciate it," he added pointedly for Evie's benefit.

The Russian nodded. "If you need time away from Utopia to spend with Miss Bishop, then I believe your cousin Ethan is now back in England."

Ian wasn't even going to bother asking how Nikolai knew that when he hadn't. "I'll call him." Maybe. Ethan could sometimes be as hotheaded as Evie was now proposing to be.

"I also want to thank you, Mr. Volkov." Evie now felt decidedly uncomfortable at her lack of manners toward the Russian. After all, the man had taken time away from his wife and baby daughter to come here. "You've been very kind."

Nikolai's expression softened as he looked at her. "I realize listening to Ian's warning of caution is not what your instinct tells you to do, but you really should do so on this matter. Cezar Fescaru is not someone you should trifle with."

All the more reason, in Evie's opinion, why she couldn't just leave Adam to their mercy.

No matter what he had done to deserve it.

CHAPTER 9

"What were you doing in my bed this morning?"
Evie had decided, while Ian was out of the room escorting
Nikolai to the door, that her best form of defense was attack.
Because she was not going to be stopped or diverted from
finding Adam. By anyone.

Ian raised mocking brows, as if he knew exactly what
she was doing. "The new couch wasn't as comfortable as it
looked."

"And you thought that gave you the right to get into
bed with me?"

"I thought I needed a decent night's sleep after only
managing to snatch two hours yesterday morning, yes."

"I didn't ask you to come to the library yesterday."

"You said you needed help finding Adam."

"You said you couldn't give it."

"I changed my mind."

"How was I to know that?"

"Evie, are you deliberately trying to antagonize me?"

Guilty color warmed her cheeks. "No, of course not."

"You know." Ian leaned back against the breakfast bar, arms folded in front of his bare chest. "Considering how everyone, including me, has gone out of their way to assist you in finding Adam, your present attitude shows a distinct lack of gratitude for that help."

"I—"

"Pick an argument with me, by all means. I have broad enough shoulders. I can take it." He shrugged. "But what did you think you were you doing, talking to Nikolai in that disrespectful way, after he left his wife and daughter to come all the way across the city to see you?"

Her shame deepened.

"Also, what the hell are you wearing?"

"I… What?" Evie gave him a sharp glance at this sudden change of topic.

"I asked what you're wearing." Ian pushed away from the breakfast bar, his gaze raking critically over her appearance. "You never dress like that."

"Like what, exactly?"

"To be noticed."

Her chin rose. "There's nothing wrong with what I'm wearing."

"Isn't there?"

Evie looked down at herself. Admittedly the jeans were a little tighter than she usually wore them, but they were clean and ironed. As for the pink vest top… It was a little more revealing than she normally wore, but she happened to like wearing it. Besides, it was cool and feminine. Truth be told, she hadn't wanted Nikolai Volkov to see her as someone who was *boring and predictable*, when the Russian would have drawn his own conclusions regarding the relationship between her and Ian.

"What I wear or do not wear is none—"

"—of my business," Ian finished in a hard voice, his arms falling back to his sides. "I'm getting a little tired of you telling me that. It's barely eight thirty on a Sunday morning, and I already feel exhausted by this constant conflict between us."

"Then—"

"Do not tell me to fuck off again either." His eyes were that dark and dangerous black Evie knew to be wary of.

She winced. "Then stop telling me what to do."

"When it's for your own good? No, not going to happen," he bit out decisively. "Volkov is a serious bad-ass who survived growing up on the streets of Moscow. His loyalty to the Markovic family is unshakable. For some reason, he has a friendship of sorts with my cousins and has helped them out on several occasions. Since I started working at Utopia, he seems to have accepted me too. But don't ever—and I mean ever—underestimate what that man is capable of."

Evie felt a shiver run down the length of her spine. She had known Nikolai Volkov was dangerous before she went to Utopia on Friday evening. With Ian here today, she had forgotten to be in awe of the other man. Because she had known Ian wouldn't let Nikolai do anything to hurt her.

Right now, she could feel the frustration coming off Ian in waves. But even as she sensed that, it began to change and grow to other churning emotions, ones she could see reflected in his eyes.

Emotions that caused the flush in her cheeks to deepen, her skin to tingle and feel sensitized, and caused the hairs on her bare arms to stand on end. There was a clenching deep inside her which grew in intensity the longer she stared into the dark depths of Ian's eyes. A sexual energy pulsed between the two of them, electrifying the air around them, so that it seemed all either of them could see was each other.

It was overwhelming.

It also threatened to swallow her whole, so that nothing and no one else mattered but Ian.

She couldn't do this again. It would break her—

"Don't." He stepped closer, the heat from his bare chest and the heady aroma of his male musk instantly invading her senses and making it difficult to breathe. "Don't go there, Evie," he murmured softly, his hand gentle against her hair. "Not now. We've both had a shitty couple of days. I'm short on sleep, and I can't stand to see you flinch away from me again right now."

That was some admission from a man who never admitted to any emotions other than sexual ones. "It isn't you." She shook her head. "It's—"

"Please don't say it's you, like one of those bad cliché breaking-up speeches."

"We can't break up when we've never been together," she dismissed.

"Stop being so damned defensive and admit that whatever was between us three years ago is still there. Because I know damn well you can feel it too." He took her hand in his and placed it against the burning heat of his chest.

Of course Evie could feel it. She had done so the moment she saw him again at Utopia. Whatever attraction—madness—had brought them together last time, it was very much still there. On her side, at least. Ian seemed to be saying it was still there for him too.

"You asked me why I was in your bed when you woke up this morning," he continued softly. "I was there because after you went to bed last night, I lay in the darkness of the sitting room for over two hours, so bloody tired I ached. I desperately needed to fall asleep, but all I could see and feel every time I closed my eyes was you. The heat and softness of you. The way you snuggle your ass against me when I cuddle you from behind. The snuffling noise you make when you turn over and press your nose against my chest."

"I do not!" It was only a halfhearted protest.

"Yeah, you do," Ian murmured indulgently. "I wanted that, Evie. I wanted it so bad, I could taste it. I could taste you. I couldn't stay away any longer. I fooled myself I only meant to look at you while you slept— Yeah I'm aware that sounds a little creepy, but you really do look cute when you're asleep," he defended as she gave a snort. "Except once I was there, beside your bed, I couldn't leave again. I was careful not to wake you as I got beneath the covers, and I had every intention of leaving before you woke up this morning."

"Except you didn't."

Ian sighed. "I fell asleep almost as soon as I cuddled up to you. I was still there when you woke up. I don't think I'd moved all night." It was the best night's sleep he'd had for... A long time. Was three years a long time? Probably, he conceded. "It was wrong of me, and I accept that I took advantage of the situation. But I give you my word I didn't take advantage of you."

She laughed softly. "I know that."

"How?"

She snorted her derision. "Do you really imagine I could ever sleep through you making love to me? Please!" All laughter left her face. "I'm tired too, Ian. Tired of dealing with Adam's behavior. Most of all, I'm tired of the two of us fighting." She moved her hands on his shoulders. "I would much rather we made love than continued to fight."

All the air whooshed from Ian's lungs, leaving him feeling light-headed and not altogether sure he'd heard her correctly. "But you're angry with me."

"Not anymore."

"That was quick."

"I'm a woman of mercurial moods," she teased.

"No, you're not."

"No, I'm not," she conceded. "But I really am so weary of the fighting."

"What about Adam?"

She sighed deeply. "If what Nikolai says is true, and Adam really is working voluntarily for the Fescarus, then he doesn't sound in any immediate danger. Delaying going to him by another hour or two isn't going to make any difference to him."

"If Nikolai says that's the way it is, then it is," Ian said with certainty.

"I know," Evie accepted heavily. "Where did I go wrong with Adam, do you think?"

He grimaced. "I believe that's the universal question of all parents who find they have created a monster by overindulgence and continually making excuses for the behavior of their offspring."

Tears pooled in Evie's eyes as she looked at him. "Adam is a mess, isn't he."

"Yes." There was no point in Ian lying about it or even trying to soften the blow. Adam Bishop was a fuckup, and a selfish bastard who had finally pissed off the wrong people, and he was now paying the price for that mistake. He had also taken up enough of Evie's thoughts and emotions for one morning. "Are you wearing a bra beneath that top?"

Her cheeks blazed with color. "The straps show if I do."

"There aren't any straps showing now."

"No."

Which meant she wasn't wearing a bra. "Are you trying to kill me?" Ian groaned, slowly pulling the tank top out of the waistband of her jeans so that his fingers could caress the warm, silky flesh of her abdomen. The soft pad of his thumbs stroked the underside of bare, uptilting breasts.

"I've called a ceasefire for the moment," she conceded huskily.

"Good." Ian claimed her lips with his own. Her taste was intoxicating, effervescent, like an expensive champagne that went straight to his head and other parts of his body.

But he wasn't interested in his own aching arousal right now, wanted only to explore and claim every inch of Evie's mouth as his own.

He stroked his tongue along the length of hers and felt her body quiver in reaction. He was rewarded with more of that trembling as he licked and tasted that warm cavern for long and pleasurable minutes.

The stroke of Evie's tongue was a swirl of pleasure curling about his. Wet and hot, in the same way her pussy would feel wrapped about his cock.

Desire wove its spell about the two of them, igniting a wild passion that surged and swelled. Only the sound of their ragged breathing filled the expectant air when Ian broke the kiss to trail his lips across her cheek, over the delicate shell of her ear, and then down the creamy column of her throat.

He could see her breasts as his lips moved lower to the bare swells visible above the tank top. Swollen nipples pressed against the soft cotton material, begging to be touched and played with. Ian cupped a hand beneath one of them as he suckled that turgid bud into his mouth, gently as he heard her initial gasp and then with increasing suction as Evie began to tremble and shake in reaction. His arms tightened about her as she gave low groan of pleasure and her nipple swelled in his mouth.

Her tank top was satisfyingly wet by the time Ian's mouth released her nipple and he raised his head. "Can we take this off?" He didn't wait for her answer as he clasped the bottom of the top and pulled it up and over her head. "You are so beautiful," he groaned as he cupped both her breasts in his hands before kissing each of the bare nipples in turn.

Evie thanked God for the genes, probably passed on by her mother, which allowed her breasts to be firm and upstanding despite their size. Her nipples were a deep rose color as Ian rolled them between his thumbs and index fingers. She closed her eyes as a river of pleasure coursed through her and caused a flood of wet and aching, swelling heat between her thighs.

Fitted jeans suddenly felt *too* tight as her clitoris and labia swelled in response to that pleasure. That pressure was relieved a little when Ian unfastened the top button and zip on her jeans before his hand slipped beneath the lace of her panties.

"God, your naked mound feels so fucking sexy," Ian groaned raggedly as his fingers parted her folds to stroke along the swollen lips. "It's like touching wet silk."

Evie was too aroused to feel embarrassed. Besides, she couldn't think of or feel anything else as Ian's fingers swirled softly and then more firmly over her clitoris and wet folds. "If you stop now, I may just have to kill you after all," she warned achingly, those pulses of pleasure deepening inside her.

Ian chuckled huskily. "I'm not going to stop, Evie. I never wanted—want to stop," he corrected gruffly as his mouth returned to pleasuring her breasts.

Evie gasped as she felt a finger breach and then enter the welcoming heat of her sheath, the muscles there contracting in response. That first finger was joined by a second, the soft pad of Ian's thumb now stroking and pressing the throb of her clit.

It was all too much. Ian was too much. He always had been.

"Let go," he encouraged, his breath hot against her wet nipple. "I'm here. I won't let you fall."

She gave a choked laugh. "I wouldn't be in this state at all if you weren't here— Oh God..." Pleasure exploded and then throbbed and swelled through her whole body, from her head to her toes, when Ian curved his fingers and stroked the knot of nerves inside her at the same time as his mouth drew hard on her nipple.

She felt the release of her juices, those spurts wetting his fingers and the intensity of her release continuing to crest and swell in never-ending waves of such intense pleasure, she remained standing only by clutching on to Ian's bare shoulders.

"Only me, Evie!" he rasped harshly as he pulled his fingers out and rubbed that wetness all over her pussy lips before raising his fingers and putting them in his mouth and slowly licking off all her juices. "God, you taste so good," he groaned. "Tell me you only come like that for me and no one else."

"No one else, Ian," she repeated obediently, her body still racked with the aftershocks of her release. "Just you."

His eyes were dark and gleaming. "Don't fucking lie to me."

"I'm not." How could she have responded to anyone else like this when Ian had been her only lover? When his touch was the only one she knew? The only one she had ever wanted.

She hadn't been with anyone else in the past three years. She might not know a lot about lovemaking, but she knew enough to know what she and Ian shared was special. That whether Ian realized it or not, whether he was willing to admit it or not, their responses to each other, the physical compatibility they had shared from the first, was rare and amazing. Even though Ian was no longer in her life, Evie hadn't been willing to accept second best. That wouldn't have been fair to the other man or her.

It wasn't special or rare enough for Ian to stay with me, a little voice taunted inside her head.

Go away, she instantly retaliated.

She wasn't a fool. Nor was she about to lie to herself. She and Ian had here and now. Evie was willing to accept that, because she had no choice but to do so.

"Only you," she repeated softly.

"Let's go to the bedroom. I want you lying down when I lick and eat the cream from your pussy." Ian swung her up into his arms to stride down the hallway to her bedroom.

Evie watched him through half-closed lids as he placed her on the bed before taking off his own jeans and boxers. His cock stood up thick and long from the thatch of dark curls at its base.

"Lift up," Ian instructed before pulling off Evie's jeans. "I thought so." He devoured her with his eyes as he looked at the pink thong she was wearing. Her bare mound was visible either side of the thin ribbon of lace. "That stays on for the moment." He moved onto the bed to kneel between her parted thighs before pulling that scrap of material to one side to reveal her pussy in all its naked glory.

Her labia were so flushed and swollen, he could clearly see the slickness of her vulva, the red nubbin above peeping out from beneath its protection hood.

Mine, came the unbidden thought.

Mine *for now*, he instantly corrected as he lifted Evie's legs and placed one over each of his shoulders before lowering his head and taking full possession of her pussy with his mouth.

It was sexy as hell as he continued to hold that lace aside as he greedily licked and lapped up the cream from Evie's release. Sweet and salty. Just the way he remembered it. Remembered her. Evie's taste was unique to her, more sweet than salty. As she was.

Had been, he corrected ruefully. This Evie felt no compunction about putting him firmly in his place when she took exception to something he said or did.

"Have you gone on strike down there?"

Or something he didn't do.

He gave her a hard grin before parting the slick rose of her pussy lips with his fingers, hearing the hitch in Evie's breath as he slowly stroked his tongue in and out of the tightness of her sheath. Seeking out and finding that sensitive knot of nerves inside her.

"Ian. Oh God, Ian." Her fingers clutched at the bedcovers beneath her as she arched her hips up to meet those moist thrusts.

"I want to see you when you come." He sat back on his haunches to watch two of his fingers thrusting in and out of her grasping pussy, using his other hand to stroke and manipulate her swollen clit until it throbbed and pulsed beneath those caresses. "Come for me now, Evie," he instructed firmly, thrusting his fingers deeper than before as he used his other hand to pinch her clit.

The sensation of Evie's second release was so intense, she became lost in a swirling vortex of emotions. The pleasure was so intense, it bordered on pain, seeming as if it turned her inside out and then pulled her back again.

And all the time it did, Ian watched her, satisfaction gleaming in those dark and fathomless eyes.

Evie was too lost in the pleasure to feel in the least vulnerable. Or to do more than groan as Ian removed her thong and then rolled a condom onto his cock before placing the swollen tip questioningly against her pussy lips. Her answer was to lift her hips and take that mushroomed top completely inside her. "More," she encouraged as he held himself back.

Ian wished he didn't have to wear a condom, would much rather have felt the bare wet heat of Evie's sheath wrapped around his cock.

She was so hot that heat permeated even the latex as he pushed slowly inside her, stretching her until she had taken the full length of him inside her. "Okay?" He moved down to lean on his elbows so that he could frame her face with his hands as he looked deeply into those sapphire-colored eyes. "Not too much?"

She smiled at him as she wrapped her arms about his

shoulders. "It's perfect."

That was how Ian felt too. This, being inside Evie, was fucking perfect. Unimagined bliss. Over the years, he had wondered if his memory had exaggerated how good it felt to be with Evie like this. It hadn't. His cock could have been sculpted to fit perfectly inside her, the walls of her sheath contracting and relaxing to draw him even deeper as he began to thrust his hips slowly forward, and then pulled back with that same slow excruciating pleasure.

"Look at us." He had lifted up to gaze down to where their bodies were joined, the dark thatch of his pubic hair appearing even darker against her bare and baby-soft mons. Watching his own cock slowly enter that slick flesh, stretching her, possessing her, was the most erotic thing he had ever seen in his life. "Look, Evie," he encouraged gruffly as he pulled one of the pillows beneath her head so that she could sit up higher still.

Evie stared down and watched as Ian's wet cock slowly withdrew from the swollen lips of her vulva. She gasped as he thrust back forcefully, stretching and filling her almost to the point of pain. That silky hardness stroked against her exposed clit with every powerful thrust.

She could feel her climax starting to build inside her as Ian continued those slow and leisurely thrusts, filling her completely before slowly withdrawing and leaving her feeling empty and longing for more. Over and over again, until Evie didn't think she could stand the torment another moment longer.

"Stop teasing me, damn you." She hit his shoulders with her clenched hands.

"Tell me what you want, Evie." His wet tongue swirled across and around her hardened nipples. "Say it out loud."

"Stop playing and take me!"

"Say it, Evie." His muscles were taut, his jaw clenched as he held himself poised above her. "Tell me exactly what you want. How you want it."

"I want you," she groaned. "Taking me. Hard."

"Whatever you want." His eyes glittered darkly as his hands moved to grasp her hips, his mouth claiming hers while his thrusts grew stronger and deeper.

Each drag of his cock over and against that sensitized knot of nerves inside her caused Evie to groan and quake, and she strained beneath him to get closer still. Reaching for, demanding their release, while he continued to hold it just out of their grasp.

Ian gasped as Evie broke the kiss to bite down on his shoulder, the rhythm of their joining instantly becoming wild, out of control. Flesh slapped against flesh. Muscles straining as they both hurtled toward their climax.

That release hit with the force of a tsunami as Ian's cock

hardened and then began to pulse its hot seed.

The storm of their mutual release swept all behind it, giving Evie no choice but to ride the crest of that wave as it took her higher and higher before hurling her into the vortex.

CHAPTER 10

"Jesus, Evie, you scared the shit out of me." Ian was staring worriedly at Evie's face when her lids fluttered open seconds later. "I thought I'd killed you."

She chuckled tiredly. "Is it possible to die from too much pleasure? If so, I'm dead."

"You feel very much alive to me," Ian assured her as he lay down beside her and pulled her snugly into his arms. Evie instantly buried her face against his chest. "But you had me worried there for a minute or two." The same two minutes he had used to dispose of the condom and wipe the excess cum off his only slightly deflated cock. He could go again, but he didn't think Evie was up to another out-of-body experience quite yet.

He wasn't sure he was either, despite the enthusiasm of his cock. He had never come so much and so hard in his life before. Once it started, it just kept coming, seeming to be dragged up from his balls in red-hot spurts that had threatened to blow the top of his head off.

Because this wasn't the Evie he had known. This was a

different, more aggressive and demanding Evie. It had been as if a bomb had gone off inside him when she sank her tiny white teeth into his shoulder and didn't let go. The pleasure and the pain had sent shock waves through his whole body, and he had just kept pumping and pumping inside her until he realized she had stilled beneath him.

That had never happened before.

They had never been that aggressive with each other before.

"Ooh ouch." Evie ran her fingertips lightly over the teeth marks on his shoulder. "Did I do that?" Her face was red with embarrassment.

"The new and bad Evie did. The good Evie would never have done such a thing." He looked at her blushing face. "Which one are you now?"

"Does it hurt?" she avoided answering him.

"Yes." No point in lying. Evie had bitten him so hard, she had broken the skin. It hurt like a motherfucker and was going to leave a bruise in the shape of Evie's teeth. Maybe even a scar.

"Then right now I'm the contrite Evie." She pulled out of his arms to sit up. "Should I get some antiseptic to put on it?"

His brows rose. "Do you have rabies?"

"I'm pretty sure I don't, no."

"Then it's fine."

"But—"

"I was shot at on a regular basis in the army," he dismissed. "I've been shot several times in the last five years too. A couple of them even put me in the hospital for a few days."

Evie had noticed several scars on his body that hadn't been there before, noticeably one on his back and another on his left pectoral muscle. "Why do you do it?" She trailed her fingertips across the ragged edges of that scar.

He shrugged. "Someone has to fight the bad guys."

She smiled slightly. "That's your superhero complex talking."

"If you say so."

Evie looked at him searchingly, sensing there was more behind that comment but knowing better than to ask Ian what it was. He had never liked talking about himself. She only knew of his five cousins, the four Knight brothers and their married sister, because Ian worked with the former. He'd also admitted that both his parents were still alive, but Evie knew he rarely visited them. She sensed there was more behind that too but knew better than to pry. She knew from experience Ian would only shut her out completely if she tried to probe too deeply into a subject he had made it clear he would rather not talk about.

She gave a self-conscious chuckle as her stomach chose that moment to rumble hungrily. "I think it's time we fed a different appetite." She climbed off the bed to pull on her robe before tying the belt securely about her waist. "Do you still like your eggs over easy and your bacon crisp?"

"And plenty of—"

"Well-cooked toast," she finished knowingly and then regretted it as she saw the sudden wariness in Ian's eyes. She gave an impatient shake of her head. "It's all right for you to know every inch of my body and for me to know every inch of yours, but not that you like your toast just shy of burned?"

Ian admitted it did sound pretty stupid, and yet, for a moment there, he'd balked at Evie knowing him well enough to remember how he liked his eggs, bacon, and toast.

It was totally illogical after the intimacies the two of them had shared only minutes ago.

And yet those feelings of panic had still been there, however briefly.

"After we've eaten, I'm going down to Canary Wharf to find the warehouse belonging to the Fescaru family."

Ian scowled at the mere idea of Evie walking into that viper's den. "And how do you intend doing that?"

"I'm pretty sure their warehouse will be the one with

the armed and muscle-bound men standing guard outside."

"Oh, very funny." Ian scowled as he sat on the edge of the bed to pull on his boxers and jeans before standing up. "You aren't going anywhere. I'm going to make some inquiries, learn exactly what the setup is there, and then *I'm* going to talk to the Fescarus on your behalf."

Her chin rose. "I don't think so."

"You aren't *thinking* at all." His hands were clenched at his sides. "As you weren't the night you walked so innocently into Utopia." He shuddered to think what might have happened if he hadn't been there and Nikolai had. He very much doubted Volkov would have made allowances for Evie's aggressive naiveté as Ian had. "Evie, let me do this for you." He forced a reasoning tone. "I know how to talk to these people." Maybe. The Fescarus were a law—or not—unto themselves.

Evie knew Ian was only trying to protect her, and in a way, it was sweet of him to want to do that—another part of that superhero complex? But this was her problem to deal with. As Adam was her problem and not Ian's.

She was still dismayed at the amount of trouble Adam had gotten himself into, was starting to wonder if gambling and computer hacking were his only vices. Although God knows those two were bad enough. Evie had absolutely no idea how she was going to extricate her twin from this mess, but she accepted it was her mess to deal with. Ian had already helped her enough.

"I can't." She refused his offer as she crossed the bedroom to the door. "I'll go and make your breakfast."

"Thanks for your help and the fuck, but now you can be on your way?"

Evie felt her face pale as she spun back to face Ian. "I didn't say that."

"You might as well have." His eyes glittered in dark challenge.

She drew in several deep breaths before answering him. Ian was spoiling for a fight, and she wasn't about to give him one. Not today. "Don't put words in my mouth."

"I'd like to put something— Never mind." His scowl deepened. "I'm not leaving here knowing you're going looking for Fescarus the moment I do. The Romanians eat little girls like you for breakfast." He attempted to reason with her.

"I'm hardly a girl!"

"No, you're a fucking librarian." He began to prowl the bedroom, his movements as gracefully predatory as the big cat he resembled. "Maybe you should start remembering that and realize this is my world, not yours."

It wasn't the first time he had made that comment. "Is that yet another reason you left three years ago, because I don't *fit into* your world?"

"What the—?" He sighed. "Evie, let's not cloud this situation with the past."

"Why not, when it also seems to be the present?" She angled her chin stubbornly. "Or did I imagine you making love to me a few minutes ago?"

Ian ran a frustrated hand through the thickness of his hair. "Don't go there, Evie."

"I am sick and tired of you telling me that." Her hands were clenched. "I didn't invite you back into my life, Ian, you walked back in voluntarily."

"Because you're so fucking naïve you were going to get yourself killed!"

"I still might." She nodded. "But that's my choice to make, not yours. I think you should go," she added heavily. "Before one or both of us says something we might seriously regret."

Ian already regretted the whole of the past forty-eight hours.

His life was structured. Deliberately so. He had his work if he required excitement, and his cousins and other friends he could spend time with if he wanted company. Which he rarely did.

Then Evie had walked into Utopia and turned that well-ordered life upside-fucking-down.

Again.

He didn't need this shit messing up his head as well as his life.

"Fine." He nodded tersely. "Forget breakfast, I'm not hungry." He brushed past her to stride through to the sitting room. He pulled on his T-shirt before sitting on the couch to put on and lace his boots.

Evie blinked back the tears as she stood in the doorway watching Ian dress in preparation for leaving. Knowing, by the finality of his tone a few minutes ago, despite the explosive lovemaking they had shared, he wouldn't be coming back this time either.

His eyes were cold as he rose back to feet. "Try not to get yourself killed, hmm?"

She shook her hair back defiantly. "As if you care!"

Ian crossed the room quietly to come to a halt mere inches in front of her. One of his hands moved up to lightly caress her cheek before dropping back to his side. "If you need me, my cell phone number is the same as it was before."

She stepped aside. "I won't need you." Pride dictated she answer him in this way, because his lack of a reply to her just now meant he really didn't care.

He gave an abrupt nod before striding out into the hallway. The apartment door closed behind him seconds later.

Evie's knees gave out, sobs racking her body as she sank to the carpeted floor and cried as if her heart were breaking.

Which it was.

Again.

"What was so urgent you had to drag me out of bed on a Sunday morning?"

"I offered to come to you." Ian opened his apartment door wider as invitation for his cousin Ethan to enter, closing the door behind the other man before they both went through to the kitchen.

Ethan gave a wicked grin as he sprawled out on one of the chairs around the kitchen table. "I don't think my date from last night would have appreciated the extra company." At the age of thirty-five, Ethan's sex life was legendary.

"Not into threesomes, huh?" Ian poured them both a mug of coffee before sitting down opposite the other man. "Or weren't you up for the competition?"

"Ha-de-ha, very funny." Ethan grinned. He was as dark-haired as Ian, but his eyes were a hazel mixture of blue, green, and brown. "So tell me your problem, and I'll see if I can help."

"What makes you think I have a problem?"

Ethan took a sip of his coffee before answering.

"Probably the fact that I've known you my whole life and this is only the second time you've invited me to your apartment."

Ian snorted. "That's bullshit, and you know it."

His cousin raised his brows. "So tell me all these occasions when I've been here. Nice apartment, by the way. A bit stark for my tastes, but I could live with it."

"You'll never have to," Ian reassured him dryly. "And you were here for… No. Well, I definitely invited you over when… No, not then either." In the past ten years, he had maybe invited half a dozen people to his apartment. He didn't remember Ethan being one of them. "Exactly when did I invite you over, Ethan?"

"Must be three years ago now."

"And you still remember it?" He eyed the other man skeptically.

"It was a momentous occasion, man. Maybe not the reason for it, but I still appreciated the invite."

"What was the reason for it?"

"So we could both get drunk to help you forget the end of the relationship with the woman you'd been dating." Ethan shrugged. "You didn't say so, but I got the impression she was the one to do the dumping. I was just saying," he defended as Ian rose abruptly to his feet.

Three years ago. A woman he'd been involved with.

Getting drunk to ease the pain.

Evie.

It had to be. He'd been out of the country for three months before he met Evie, and he hadn't had a relationship with another woman before or since. A lot of one-night stands, but not a relationship.

He didn't remember the night Ethan was talking about, but then he couldn't remember how he'd spent a lot of his evenings around that time.

He sighed heavily. "She's back."

Ethan squinted up at him. "Who is?"

"The woman."

His cousin's brows rose. "She dumped you before, and you still let her back in your life?"

"I was the one who did the dumping, and she isn't back in my life."

Ethan eyed him derisively. "Do you want to try that again, cuz, 'cause your voice rose up pretty high toward the end there. As in, you're protesting too much and too loudly."

Ian began to pace the kitchen. "Involving you was a mistake."

Ethan watched him for several minutes before speaking again. "What do you want me to do? Tell her to go away politely? Beg on your behalf? Name it, and I'll see what I can do."

Ian stared at him. "Why the hell would I ask you to do either of those things? And why would you *do* any of those things for me?"

"Because we're family, man." Ethan frowned. "It's what families do for each other."

"No." Ian shook his head. "No, it's really not."

"It's what our family does," his cousin insisted. "You were all there for us after our parents died, so I'm here for you. Any time. Whatever you want."

All there for them. Ian's parents. Ian. And—

"What I want is for you to guard someone without them knowing you're doing it," Ian bit out abruptly.

"I can do that, no problem." Ethan nodded. "The woman?"

"Yes."

"Who does she need guarding against?"

"The Romanian mafia."

Ethan straightened in the chair. "Jesus Christ, Ian, who the hell is this woman?"

"A librarian."

"A...? No." Ethan shook his head. "If you want me to do this, then you have to be honest with me."

"I am being honest." Ian grimaced. "She's a librarian, and her brother is a douche bag working for the Romanians. She has it in her head she needs to save him. From himself, if necessary."

He had come up with the idea of Ethan guarding Evie once he was back in his own apartment and could think straight again without Evie's presence to confuse the issue. She had made it clear she didn't want him around anymore, and he had left her with a "call me if you need me," something he knew Evie's pride would never allow her to do. Once home, he'd remembered Nikolai had told him Ethan was back, and asking his cousin to protect Evie seemed like a good compromise.

"Is she beautiful?"

Ian didn't even attempt to misunderstand his cousin's question. "Very," he confirmed grimly.

"Sexy?"

"I think so." Hell, Evie's sexiness brought him to his knees every fucking time. As for how she'd looked in that pink tank top earlier... Ian had wanted to wrap her up in a blanket and not let anyone else—any other man—see her wearing it.

"Does she feel the same way about you?"

His eyes narrowed. "And what way is that?"

"She's beautiful, sexy, you get this possessive gleam in your eyes when you talk about her. If she feels the same way about you..."

"She doesn't," Ian stated flatly. "I'm good for the

occasional fuck, but I don't fit into the rest of her academic life."

"That's a bit harsh."

"To her or to me?"

"Both."

"Let's try and stay on subject, hmm, Ethan?"

"Which is making sure she doesn't fall into the hands of the Fescarus?"

He nodded. "She's dead set on saving her brother. If she even attempts to go near the Fescaru warehouse, I want you to call me immediately."

Ethan winced. "When she does something, she really goes for the top, doesn't she. Or the bottom, depending on your point of view." He gave a grimace of distaste for the Romanian family.

"You have no idea."

"You want me to start now?"

Ian grinned his relief that his cousin was agreeable to helping him. "You can finish your coffee first."

Ethan chuckled. "Your generosity knows no bounds."

Ian sobered. "I don't want any of your brothers or Knight Security brought in on this. It stays between the two of us."

"Are you kidding?" The other man snorted. "My brothers are so busy with their wives, they don't have a clue what's going on around them anymore."

"Do I detect a note of jealousy in your voice?" Ian mocked.

"No way!" Ethan scorned. "I love and respect all my sisters-in-law, but I owe it to all the other beautiful women in the world to ensure one of the Knight brothers remains available."

He chuckled. "You really believe that."

"Of course. Now fill me in on all the details, and I'll get started."

Ian chose to ignore the voice in his head telling him this was a bad idea, and that Evie was going to be truly pissed if she realized Ian had arranged a bodyguard for her. Well, that was just too bad, because there was no way Ian could really walk away and leave her to her own devices. She had always been blindly loyal to her brother, but in this situation, that loyalty was beyond blind.

It was a blindness that could get her killed.

CHAPTER 11

"Who are you and why are you following me?" Evie demanded as she confronted the man she had noticed outside her apartment building earlier. He was a man neither she nor any other woman could help but notice, being tall, dark, and very handsome.

He was the same man who had then followed her on the underground. Also the man who had followed her from the train station at a safe distance as she set off to take a look at all the warehouses in this less fashionable area of the dockside.

That same distance had also allowed her to duck behind one of the buildings and wait to ambush him as he came round the corner.

"Actually, don't bother answering," she murmured now that she had a closer look at him. "Which Knight brother are you?" His resemblance to Ian in coloring and facial features was too extreme for the two men not to be related. "Actually, now that I think about it, don't bother to answer that either. You have to be Ethan, because your brothers are all on honeymoon or about to be."

Hazel eyes darkened with admiration. "Are you really a librarian?"

"I am." Although he could be forgiven for doubting that at the moment.

Evie was still wearing the fitted jeans and pink tank top, the latter beneath a short black leather jacket. An outfit Ian had claimed she would be *noticed* in. Because she wanted the Fescarus to notice her. How else was she going to breach their security and be allowed to speak with her brother?

"Librarians didn't look like you when I was at school," Ethan murmured flirtatiously.

"This is all very interesting, Mr. Knight—"

"Ethan."

"Ethan." She nodded. "But if Ian sent you to follow me, you can go straight back and tell him—"

"To fuck off or to stick his help where the sun don't shine?"

She felt the warmth of color enter her cheeks. "I see you and your cousin have had a little chat about me."

"Oh, it wasn't little." Ethan grinned.

"I'm sure it wasn't." But one thing Evie was sure of, Ian wouldn't have told his cousin everything about their relationship, past or present. "Do you know which of these warehouses belongs to the Fescarus?"

"None of them."

Her heart sank. "I'm in the wrong place?"

"You are," he confirmed.

She winced. "And you aren't going to tell me where the right place is, are you."

"No."

Her eyes narrowed. "Does Ian know their exact location too?"

"You would have to ask him that."

"Very diplomatically put, Mr. Knight."

He shrugged. "I'm well known for my diplomacy."

For all that Evie was disappointed she had apparently come to the wrong industrial site, she couldn't help but like this man. At least when Ethan told her no, he did it in such a way as not to make her feel like hitting him, unlike someone else she could mention. "Ian very rarely chooses to answer the questions I ask him."

"Maybe that's because of the questions you ask."

She spun round to find Ian standing a few feet behind her. She gave Ethan Knight a narrowed-eyed and accusing glare. He had to have known his cousin was standing behind her. "You called him."

Ethan held his hands up defensively. "I'm just following orders."

"If you had done that, she wouldn't have known you

were following her," Ian snapped impatiently as he stepped forward. "You've only been watching her for a couple of hours. What happened to guarding her without her knowing you're doing it?"

Ethan grinned unrepentantly. "Is it my fault she couldn't help but notice my magnetic good looks?"

Despite the gravity of the situation, Evie found herself holding back a smile, both at Ethan's lighthearted banter and Ian's scowling response to it.

Ian turned a challenging gaze on her. "What are you doing here, Evie?"

Her eyes widened at the iciness of Ian's tone. "You already know the answer to that."

"I also remember that I told you not to go looking for the Fescarus."

"Whoa, not a good tone or attitude, cuz," Ethan muttered under his breath as he no doubt saw the angry flush Evie could feel warming her cheeks. "No wonder she told you to fuck off and stick your opinions. In my experience, women don't react well to being given orders. Cajoling or charm, maybe, but never—"

"Butt out, Ethan," Ian growled.

Ethan turned to Evie. "I apologize for my Neanderthal cousin. But I also have to advise you it isn't a good idea to contact the Fescaru family in this direct and confrontational way. They won't appreciate it, and a woman on her own is too vulnerable. Far better that Ian or I contact them on your behalf and arrange a meeting."

It was the same advice Ian had given her, but with far less force and anger.

She concentrated on Ethan. "You would do that for me?"

He nodded. "Of course."

"Today?"

"Sure."

Ian didn't like the way this conversation was going *at all.*

Or the fact that Evie seemed willing to accept the same help from Ethan she had earlier refused from him. "*I* advise we all leave the area, before we attract the wrong attention."

"So the Fescarus' headquarters *are* around here somewhere?" Evie pounced.

"Somewhere," he bit out unhelpfully.

"Well, that's a bit of an improvement on Neanderthal man," Ethan drawled, "but still bordering on arrogant. The gist of Ian's comment is correct, though, Evie," he sobered. "We should all go and grab lunch somewhere and discuss our plan of action."

"We don't have a fucking plan of action, nor do we need one," Ian rasped. "Her brother, Adam, is twenty-six years old and working for the Fescarus voluntarily. Nor has he bothered to call Evie to let her know he's okay and not to worry about him."

"Twenty-six." Ethan's attention stayed on Evie. "Adam is your twin?"

"Yes."

"Wow, that's some coincidence—"

"Ethan, shut the fuck up," Ian snarled.

"But—"

"Don't force me into making you."

"You think you could?" Ethan challenged. "Underneath this affable nature is a ninja waiting to be set free," he confided in Evie. "Besides, I don't see what the problem is with Evie knowing—" He didn't get to finish the sentence because Ian's fist landed on his jaw and knocked him off his feet.

"My God…" Evie gasped as she went down on her knees beside a prone Ethan. "Are you okay?" she prompted worriedly.

He rubbed his bruised jaw as he sat up. "Fine."

She glared up at Ian. "What the hell is wrong with you?"

"*You're* what's wrong with me." His hands were still clenched into fists at his sides. "Your recklessness is driving me insane."

Tears stung her eyes as she sat back on her heels. "Go away, Ian. Please, just go away."

"And if I choose not to?"

She sighed wearily. "If you won't go, then I obviously can't make you." She stood up before holding out a hand to help Ethan back onto his feet. "But if you're going to stay, I have to be the one to leave," she added coldly. "Because right now, I can't even stand to look at you. Oh and you might want to apologize to your cousin sometime today." She turned to the other man. "Nice to have met you, Ethan."

He nodded. "You too, Evie."

"Where are you going?" Ian called after her as she walked away.

She didn't even bother to glance back as she answered him. "As far from you as possible!"

"Well, that went well," Ethan drawled. "And just so you know, if you hit me again, I'm going to retaliate," he warned in an icy-cold voice completely unlike his usual light-hearted banter.

"I'm not going to hit you again," Ian dismissed, still watching Evie as she walked back toward the railway station.

"An apology *would* be appropriate."

"I apologize."

"Like to try that again, but with more sincerity?" Ethan quirked dark brows. "I've been known to break an arm or two for far less than what you just did to me."

Ian knew the other man wasn't kidding about his ninja abilities. Ethan was a black belt in several of the martial arts.

"Care to explain why you hit me the first time?" his cousin prompted. "Although I'm guessing it had something to do with stopping me from mentioning Sophie?"

Ian's mouth tightened. "You know I never talk about the past."

"You don't talk about the future either." Ethan shrugged. "Doesn't mean it doesn't or didn't exist. Just as Sophie existed," he added softly. "You weren't the only one who loved her, you know."

Ian could feel a nerve pulse in his tightly clenched jaw. "I'm not going there, Ethan."

"How long were you and Evie together three years ago?"

"None of your fucking business—"

"What harm can it do to tell me? Was it a day? Two days? Two weeks?" his cousin persisted. "Because you can't have spent all that time in bed together, must have had a conversation or two at some point. You seem to know quite a lot about her brother."

"We talked," Ian allowed grudgingly.

"But I'm guessing not about you?"

"No."

Ethan studied him closely. "Have you ever talked to anyone about it?"

"Like who?"

"A therapist, maybe. I went along a couple of times when Caleb was having his therapy for PTSD. Talking has helped him."

"I'm not suffering from PTSD," Ian dismissed.

"Now you're being deliberately obtuse—"

"No, I'm deliberately blocking your chosen topic of conversation. I said no, Ethan," he said harshly as his cousin would have spoken again. "Now let's get the fuck away from here. I noticed several ICTVs in the area, and if they belong to the Fescarus, they may decide to come and investigate. Do you want a lift home?"

"What about Evie?"

His mouth thinned. "You can leave Evie to me." It had seemed like a good idea to involve Ethan at the time, but for those few hours Ethan had been watching her, it had been impossible for Ian to do anything but pace up and down and worry about her. He might as well worry while keeping watch in her apartment as sitting alone in his own apartment doing the same thing.

"In that case, I have a lady friend who lives not far from here on Canary Wharf." Ethan gave one of his cheeky grins. "No doubt she'll be happy to offer me some TLC for my bruised jaw."

"Is that what you call it, TLC?"

"Whatever." His cousin's grin widened. "I like your Evie, by the way. Ballsy lady."

"Yes, she is." But she wasn't Ian's.

In fact, after his behavior today, he doubted Evie would want to speak to him again, let alone have him in her apartment. "I really am sorry for hitting you, Ethan. I was just... It was…"

"It's all good, cuz," Ethan dismissed. "Now I should follow your lady home before she decides to do something else she shouldn't."

Good advice.

Except Evie wasn't *at* home. At least she wasn't answering the intercom when Ian buzzed up to her apartment twenty minutes later.

He stood back from the building to look up at the third floor. Not that he could see very much. It wasn't as if Evie was going to be conveniently standing at one of the windows looking down at him.

He rang the intercom again. And then again. And again. If he made enough of a nuisance of himself, she would probably answer, if only so she could tell him what she thought of him.

Except she didn't.

Not even when he kept his finger on the intercom buzzer for a full minute.

She wasn't answering her cell phone either.

Which meant she was either totally pissed with him and deliberately wasn't answering her door or cell phone, or she wasn't at home and had no access to her cell phone.

The uneasy feeling in the pit of Ian's stomach told him it was the latter.

That she had never returned from Canary Wharf.

"I don't appreciate being brought here against my will." Despite her outwardly confident demeanor, Evie's knees were trembling as she looked across the width of the desk at the man seated behind it.

A man she could only assume had the surname Fescaru. Assume, because he hadn't bothered introducing himself when she'd been brought to him at gunpoint a few minutes ago.

She had waited only as long as it took Ian and Ethan to become preoccupied in what looked like an intense conversation before ducking out of sight behind one of the warehouses. After that, it was just a question of waiting until the two men had left the area, Ian in his car, Ethan walking off in the direction of the luxury apartment buildings on Canary Wharf.

There were two small industrial estates in this area, backing onto each other, and after Ian's comment that the Fescaru warehouse was "somewhere" nearby, Evie had decided if this was the wrong one, then there was a pretty good chance the other one was the right one.

Which had proven to be the case when, within minutes of her entering the area of what mainly looked to be deserted warehouses, she found herself face-to-face with a man sporting a lot of defined muscles emphasized by the cut of his suit and pointing a gun at her as he gave her a leering smile.

He hadn't spoken a word to her as he jerked the gun to the right as indication he wanted her to precede him. Evie's questions as to who he was and what he wanted with her— as if she didn't know that already—had gone unanswered.

He'd brought her up some steps inside one of the warehouses and shown her into the office where this man was seated behind the desk. A swarthy man probably aged in his mid-fifties, slightly overweight, with iron-gray hair brushed back from his face.

He leaned back in his chair to look at her with cold, dark eyes between narrowed lids. "I was told you came willingly."

She nodded. "But only because your man had a gun." She glanced back to where two men, one the gun-wielding guy from earlier, stood guard beside the door into the office. "I want to speak to my brother," she added challengingly as she turned back to the older man.

"Your brother?"

"Adam Bishop."

Something flickered in the man's dark gaze and then was as quickly masked. "I know no one of that name."

Liar, liar, pants on fire.

Evie knew she hadn't imagined that brief moment of recognition when she said her brother's name. "I only want to see him, reassure myself that he's okay, and then I'll leave." She hated the sound of pleading in her voice, but she doubted threats would hold much sway with this man.

"I told you, I know no one of that name. Now—"

"I'm not leaving until I've spoken to Adam."

"There is no one here by that name."

"I don't believe you."

Iron-gray brows rose to his hairline as if this man was unaccustomed to being questioned regarding any statement he might care to make. Which he probably was if he was a Fescaru, Evie conceded with a sickening lurch of her stomach.

"Nor am I leaving until I've spoken to my brother," she added stubbornly.

That dark gaze moved to the two men standing beside

the door. "Take Miss Bishop to one of the storerooms and see that she stays there. Ensure that you remove her bag and any mobile devices from her pockets too."

"You can't keep me a prisoner here!" Evie protested as the two men moved forward to grasp her arms.

Those dark eyes looked at her unemotionally. "You are my guest, not my prisoner."

Evie struggled against the tight hold the men had of her arms. "In the same way my brother is your *guest*?"

"I suggest you not try my patience any further with your ridiculous accusations in regard to a man I have already told you I do not know," he dismissed in a hard voice.

The two men began to drag her toward the door. "You won't get away with this," she warned. "Someone will come looking for me and—"

"The same two gentlemen who have now left the area in the belief you had done so too?" he mocked.

The *same two gentlemen* Evie had told she didn't need their protection or help.

Would either Ian or Ethan bother to check whether or not she had got home safely, or would Ian have finally accepted her dismissal of his protection and left her to her own devices?

Several hours of being locked in a storeroom and ignored, no matter how many times she banged on the door for attention, gave Evie her answer to that question.

Ian had finally taken her at her word and given up on her.

CHAPTER 12

"You're going to wear a hole in the carpet," Ethan remarked dryly as he sat in a chair observing Ian as he paced the room restlessly.

Ian ignored him as he kept pacing. It had been over two hours now since he'd gone to Evie's apartment and discovered she wasn't there. Two hours of mental torment when all sorts of scenarios had played out in his mind. He liked the one where she had gone shopping the best, but accepted that was more of a fairy tale than realism.

He *knew* Evie well enough to know that she had given up too easily earlier this morning. Something he had cursed himself repeatedly for since and should have realized at the time. As Ethan had said, Evie was a ballsy lady. Reckless to the point of stupidity where her brother was concerned, but ballsy nonetheless. All of which meant Ian should have known she wouldn't have hesitated to continue her search for both the Fescarus and her brother.

"What are we doing here exactly?" Ethan prompted at Ian's continued silence.

Here was Ian's office at Utopia. As for what they were doing here—

"I believe you are waiting to see and speak to me." A tall, dark-haired man entered the room, a familiar blond-haired man following closely behind him. "Mr. Knight." He nodded briefly in Ian's direction before looking inquiringly at Ethan.

"I'm also Mr. Knight. Ian's cousin Ethan." The two men shook hands.

"Gregori Markovic," the Russian supplied economically. "My associate Nikolai Volkov."

It had taken only a single glance at Nikolai's face for Ian to know the other man was more than a little pissed at having his Sunday disturbed for the second time in a matter of hours. Gregori didn't look too impressed by it either.

Which he really couldn't give a fuck about right now. "Evie went looking for the Fescarus," he supplied tersely. "As she is now missing, it's my belief she found them." His stomach gave that now-familiar and sickening lurch at what might have happened to her in the past two hours.

His immediate instinct on realizing Evie had disappeared had been to go directly to the Fescaru warehouse and demand to see her. His second had called for more caution. He doubted Fescaru would admit to having Evie, and Ian certainly wouldn't be helping her if he ended up becoming the Fescarus' unwilling guest too. Contacting Markovic through Nikolai had seemed the safer option, even if involving them presented its own dangers. Their displeasure toward Ian aside, a turf war between the Romanians and Russians would tear London apart.

Having considered all the other options, Ian had decided none of them were viable. After which he had telephoned Nikolai to ask for his help.

Gregori now observed him through narrowed lids. "Nikolai has explained some of the situation to me on the drive here. My question to you is what do you expect from us in regard to Miss Bishop's…dilemma?"

"Who *are* you?"

Evie frowned at the question. Having been locked in the store room for the past three hours without water or food or access to a bathroom, her throat was scratchy and sore from shouting out her protest at being imprisoned at all. She had also demanded the use of a bathroom and been granted that small concession when the two bodyguards returned a few minutes ago to escort her to back to this office.

"I already told you that earlier," she dismissed. "Perhaps you would now do me the courtesy of telling me who you are?"

His mouth twisted derisively. "As if you do not know that already!"

Arrogant bastard. "Sorry to disappoint you, but I have no idea."

He looked suitably irritated. "I am Cezar Fescaru."

Not just any Fescaru, then, but the top man himself. "Mr. Fescaru." She nodded. "Can I take it my being brought back to see you means you have decided to release my brother and me?"

"I am considering it."

The relief of knowing Adam was still alive robbed her of breath for several seconds. It was also a vast improvement on Fescaru having earlier denied all knowledge of Adam's existence. "What is there to consider?" She frowned her puzzlement at this further delay.

Cezar Fescaru gave a cold smile. "That is the reason I asked who you are."

"And I've told you I'm Adam Bishop's sister. I know Adam owes you money, and I assure you I will ensure the debt is repaid." It was an empty promise at best, but hopefully Fescaru had no idea she didn't have the money to repay him. Getting Adam away from here was all that mattered for the moment. They could deal later with the problem of how they were going to repay the money her brother owed to people like Fescaru and Markovic.

"That is all well and good." He stood up from behind his desk, revealing him as a man of average height but one who nevertheless possessed that air of arrogance his position of power gave him. "But I wish to know what your connection is to the Markovic family."

"The...?" Evie gave a puzzled shake of her head. "I don't have a connection to the Markovic family."

Fescaru's smile lacked any real humor. "Now it is my turn not to believe you."

"I assure you I don't—" She broke off as the office door opened and six men were ushered into the room, followed by two more of Fescaru's bodyguards.

The two men who instantly moved forward to flank the tall and harshly handsome man standing at the front of the group were obviously his bodyguards from their muscular physique, black suits, and shoulder holsters. Empty shoulder holsters, Evie noted with dismay, which meant these men had been disarmed before being allowed into Fescaru's office.

Ian and Ethan she obviously recognized instantly. As she did Nikolai Volkov. She had never seen the fourth man before, but after her conversation just now with Cezar Fescaru, and the presence of Nikolai Volkov and the bodyguards, she would take a guess on this being Gregori Markovic.

There was only one way that Evie could think of for the

two Russians having become involved in all this.

What had Ian *done*?

What had Evie *forced* him into doing, with her stubborn determination to seek out Cezar Fescaru and demand Adam's release?

Whatever it was, Evie couldn't read any of Ian's emotions regarding this situation from his closed expression. His mouth was thinned, his eyes cold and aloof, and he kept his face averted from looking at her directly as he stood slightly behind Gregori and Nikolai. The only reassurance she received came from Ethan, as he gave her a friendly wink.

"Markovic."

"Fescaru."

Evie's attention was instantly riveted to the front of the room as two of the most powerful men of the London underworld come face-to-face. Possibly for the first time? As it was a world Evie had no knowledge of—yes, she freely admitted that now—she had no idea if that was the case.

Despite the lack of aggression in the two men's greetings, the tension in the room was palpable.

Probably because there was too much testosterone in too small a space, Evie acknowledged with a grimace. Whatever the reason, the threat of violence seemed to simmer beneath the surface of their civility. As if a wrong move from either man could and would precipitate a bloodbath.

A bloodbath, if it happened, Evie would be completely responsible for.

"Please." She stepped forward. "I don't—"

"Take care of your woman, Knight." Nikolai barked the order without so much as looking at her as he concentrated his glacial-eyed attention on Cezar Fescaru.

Before Evie could protest, her arm was taken in a firm grasp and she was pulled to the back of the room.

Not by Ian but by Ethan.

"Not a word," he warned, his lips barely moving.

She gave a pained frown in Ian's direction, but all she could see was the tension in his back as he remained facing forward.

"It has come to my attention you have something of mine," Gregori Markovic spoke to the other man coldly. "Two somethings, to be exact."

"Do I?"

"Do not play games with me, Cezar." Markovic's voice became softer, but the threat remained as an undertone. "Bishop works for me. I want him back. Miss Bishop belongs to one of my men. He wishes for her safe return also."

Evie's eyes widened. "What—" She broke off with a

gasp as Ethan's hand tightened painfully on her arm.

"Bishop made no mention of your connection when he agreed to work for me," Fescaru drawled. "Loyalty, it is so hard to find nowadays, would you not agree?"

"No," the Russian bit out. "Now if you would return my property to me? I am to accompany my wife and son on a visit with friends this evening." In just a few words and the contempt in his tone, Markovic managed to imply he didn't consider Fescaru in that category, nor would he ever allow this man anywhere near his wife and son.

Fescaru looked unperturbed by the insult. "It is customary to make an exchange in such circumstances."

"In your country, perhaps," Gregori allowed. "But this is not your country or your city. It is mine. We have an agreement, do we not?" he challenged coldly.

Fescaru looked a little less sure of himself. "We do."

"The penalty, if your business interests ever infringe upon mine, is the expulsion of you and your men from my city."

"Yes."

The Russian nodded. "You are seriously in danger of stepping over that line in regard to both Mr. and Miss Bishop."

Fescaru looked a *lot* less sure of himself now. "I assure you it was not done intentionally."

Gregori nodded abruptly. "I am willing to overlook it this time, if that is the case."

"Marku, you will bring Mr. Bishop to my office immediately." Fescaru issued the order, and one of his bodyguards instantly left the room. "Exactly what is Mr. Bishop's role in your organization?"

Gregori looked down the length of his arrogant nose at the Romanian. "I do not consider that to be any of your business. Any more," he added softly as the other man bristled resentfully, "than it is my business what you use the warehouse in Brixton for. But I could make it so, if that is what you wish."

"That won't be necessary," the older man assured hastily.

"I thought not." Gregori gave a hard smile.

Ian wasn't sure if the room had become hotter or if it was his own body heat that had deepened. Either way, he could feel the beads of sweat on his forehead as these two men wielded their threats beneath a veneer of politeness that would crack open into a maelstrom of violence if one or both of them chose to issue the order for it to do so.

Fescaru and his bodyguards were seriously outnumbered, of course, but all the Markovic weapons had been removed before they were allowed into Fescaru's office. The Romanian was also known for being hotheaded where his pride was concerned, and at the moment, Gregori was enjoying himself a little too much at the older man's expense.

As for Evie…

Ian's heart had stopped beating the moment he walked into the room and saw her standing there, completely unharmed, thank God. Physically, at least. The flush in her cheeks and the glitter in her eyes said that her temper hadn't fared as well.

Would she never learn, never listen to him, when he told her these men were seriously dangerous to be around? That she didn't have the luxury of losing her temper with either Fescaru or Gregori?

Well, if she hadn't, Ian intended making that very clear to her, and sooner rather than later.

"Cezar, what—Evie…?" Adam Bishop came to a halt in the doorway the moment he saw his sister.

There was no concern in his expression for the fact his sister was standing in a room with two of the most powerful men in the London underworld, and that at least four of the men with them were armed.

"Adam!" Evie ran across the room to launch herself into her twin's arms. "Oh God, Adam!" Tears of relief cascaded down her cheeks as she held on to him tightly.

"What on earth are you doing here, Evie?" Adam

managed to extricate himself before holding her at arm's length. He was obviously uncomfortable with his sister's show of affection in front of so many other man.

Ian knew the exact moment the selfish little shit spotted and recognized Nikolai, because his eyes widened and his face paled slightly. Adam's wariness deepened as he looked at Gregori Markovic, and then there was another widening of his eyes as he belatedly recognized Ian.

He quickly turned away from Ian's narrow-eyed condemnation. "What's going on?"

"We are leaving now, Cezar, and taking Adam and Miss Bishop with us," Gregori informed the older man. "But understand this," he added icily. "I will not be so reasonable if anything like this happens again."

Evie felt an equally icy shiver run the length of her spine at the unmistakable threat behind those words.

But she was too happy to have Adam alive and well and leaving with them to be too concerned with how Cezar Fescaru or Gregori Markovic felt about it.

She had a feeling she was going to hear enough of that from Ian.

CHAPTER 13

"Not a single fucking word," Ian warned between clenched teeth as Evie would have turned in the passenger seat of his car and spoken to him.

A warning Evie had no intention of listening to when she required answers to several questions. "Why is Adam in the car with Gregori Markovic and not us?" She kept her gaze fixed on the two limousines ahead of Ian's car, their windows darkened so that the occupants couldn't be seen. But she knew exactly who was in both those cars.

Gregori Markovic, Adam, and two of the bodyguards were in the first car; Nikolai, Ethan, and the other two Markovic bodyguards were in the second one. Ian hadn't consulted Evie or anyone else before putting her in the passenger seat of his own car and getting in behind the wheel.

Ian glanced at her. "Do you ever listen to anything I or anyone else says to you?"

"Of course I listen—"

"And then go ahead and do whatever the fuck you

please," he bit out disgustedly. "Well, it stops now, Evie. All of it. Before you get yourself or someone else killed."

"I only wanted Adam back."

"And he was perfectly happy where he was."

"You don't know that."

"No?" Ian glanced at her. "Didn't his reluctance to leave pretty well take care of that?"

Evie's cheeks warmed at the derision in his tone. There was no denying Adam had been reluctant to leave. In fact, he had been furious with Evie for interfering. "He owes Fescaru money. He was probably frightened there would be reprisals if he left with us."

"Oh, there will most definitely be reprisals," Ian assured her softly.

She eyed him warily. "Are you saying that Gregori and Nikolai intend—"

"The reprisals won't be on Adam."

"Then who— Me?" She eyed him warily.

"You," Ian confirmed grimly.

"Gregori and Nikolai are going to punish me for wanting to save my brother?"

"No. I am."

"You— Where are they taking Adam?" she demanded, turning to look at the two limousines as they took a turn to the left and Ian kept his car on the main road. "Ian?"

"Adam has to remain with Markovic for a while. It has to be this way, Evie," he snapped as she frowned.

"Why does it? Are they going to hurt Adam?" she added anxiously.

"Gregori told Fescaru that Adam works for him. It was the only way he could request his release. Now Adam has to stay with them for a while to corroborate that claim. And no, I don't believe Gregori has any intention of hurting your brother."

It made a certain sense to Evie. Nevertheless… "So we got Adam away from the Romanian mafia and gave him to the Russian *bratva* instead."

"*You* didn't get him diddlysquat, Evie," Ian snapped. "The two of you would still be *guests* of Cezar Fescaru if it had been left to you."

That also was true. "I haven't thanked you yet for what you did. I know you must have been responsible for involving Nikolai and Gregori."

"You can save the thanks for later."

"Later? But— You missed the turnoff to my apartment!" This time she turned to look at the road they should have gone down but hadn't.

"Because you aren't going to your apartment."

"Why aren't I?"

Ian sighed his impatience with her continuous

questions. "Because your actions today also brought you to the attention of the head of the Romanian mafia. He only let you and Adam go because Markovic pressured him into doing so. But that doesn't mean Fescaru has to like it. In fact, I know he didn't." Ian wasn't going to forget the look of murderous rage in Fescaru's eyes in a hurry. "Consequently, you can't return to your apartment yet or be left unprotected either."

"So are you taking me to a hotel?"

"You would be no safer there than in your own home."

"So where are you taking me?"

He gave a hard smile. "For the moment, you will be staying at my apartment with me."

"Your apartment?"

"Yes," he bit out, hearing how surprised Evie was by his answer.

None of their nights together three years ago had been at Ian's apartment. By his design. Ethan had been right earlier; Ian didn't invite people to his apartment.

Evie shook her head. "In that case, I'm going to need to pack some of my personal things to take with me. If you could just—"

"No."

"I may not have been Fescaru's prisoner for very long, but I still need to wash the feel of that place off me and change my clothes." She gave a shudder.

"You can take a shower at my place."

"And wear what?"

"You can walk around fucking naked for all I care—
We'll pick up some of your stuff tomorrow," he relented as
she gasped. "For the moment, I have T-shirts, sweats, and
a spare robe you can wear. After which you and I are going
to discuss those *reprisals* I mentioned in greater detail." Not
only had Evie put her own life in jeopardy but those of
everyone who had been at that warehouse today.

It was time for her to learn her actions had
consequences.

Evie couldn't deny her curiosity to see Ian's apartment.
He had never invited her there in the past. It had been as
if it was some hallowed place, his own personal space, and
no one was allowed to intrude. She had assumed because it
would reveal too much about the man himself.

Except it was the complete opposite.

Admittedly, it was on the penthouse floor of a luxury
apartment building, implying he had some serious wealth
behind him. But inside, it was more like some high-class
hotel suite than someone's home.

Everything was minimalist, from color to furnishings.
The color scheme was gray and white throughout, the

furniture square and modern, with impressionist paintings on the walls. There were no ornaments or photographs anywhere. The kitchen was equally as impersonal, everything gray or white again, with chrome appliances. Everything was neatly in its place, as if no one lived here. Certainly not Ian.

It was all a characterless blur of blah, and totally unlike Ian, who she knew to be a mass of surging and extreme emotions beneath his often silent exterior.

"You can use the bedroom second door on the right," he told her. "It has an adjoining bathroom if you would like to take that shower now. I'll make sure there's some clothes in the bedroom for you to wear when you come out."

Evie needed something to eat and drink as much as she needed to shower. It seemed like a very long time ago since the coffee and toast she'd had for breakfast this morning after Ian left her apartment. She'd had nothing to eat or drink since then, just a lot of adrenaline surging through her bloodstream.

"I'll make coffee and something to eat while you're gone." Ian seemed to read her thoughts. "You'll find soap and shampoo in the cupboard under the vanity unit."

Evie eyed him warily, finding his attitude too pleasantly reasonable after his threat in the car. It made her feel uneasy, as if there was a storm brewing on the horizon but it wouldn't break until Ian was ready to let it do so.

Even so, she couldn't resist looking into the other rooms as she walked down the hallway to the bedroom and bathroom Ian had said she could use. The first room on the right was a study, but again it had modern furniture and very little character, and the top of the pine desk was completely bare.

The first open door on the left was obviously Ian's bedroom.

Well, maybe not so obviously, as the décor was still that gray and white, but unlike the other rooms, there were a few things in there that marked it as being inhabited. A shirt lying over the back of the bedroom chair, and a pair of black shoes tucked beneath it, and a pair of gold cuff links on the dresser.

There was also a photograph on Ian's bedside cabinet.

The rest of the apartment was so noticeably bare of all photographs, this one and the placement of it marked it as being significant.

She could only see the back of the photo frame, so she had no idea what or who it was a photograph of. But obviously there was someone or something he wanted to be the last thing he saw at night and the first he would see in the morning.

Ian had kissed and made love to her several times in the past three days, and Evie had assumed he wasn't involved with someone. But what if he was? What if she had been falling in love all over again with a man who was involved with someone else?

"What the hell are you doing?"

She turned in the doorway with a guilty start, her heart pounding as she saw the coldness of Ian's expression at finding her literally gawping into the privacy of his bedroom. "I— Er, so much has happened today, I forgot which bedroom you said I could use."

"Really?"

Evie winced at the lack of conviction in his tone. Deservedly so. She had known exactly which bedroom she was supposed to use but had allowed herself to be tempted by the open door of what she had realized was Ian's bedroom.

In the expectation of perhaps being given some insight into a man who seemed even more of an enigma to her now than he had in the past. Today was an example of that. Ian was obviously responsible for Gregori Markovic's intervention with Cezar Fescaru, and yet there was no gladness in him for that rescue having been successful. Only that burning anger that threatened to spiral out of control if she said or did the wrong thing.

Such as invading the privacy of his bedroom...

"Really," she confirmed evenly.

Ian put him arm across the doorway, blocking her way as she would have continued down the hallway. "If you would rather share my bedroom, then just say so."

Evie cheeks heated as she looked into challenging and mocking dark eyes. "No, thank you," she answered primly. "But I would appreciate the loan of the clothes and robe." And to have him move out of her way.

Because the heat of him and that spicy male musk were having their usual effect on her senses. Her heart was beating far too rapidly, and she could feel a nerve pulsing in her throat. Her cheeks also felt far too warm, her gaze feverish.

He stepped aside. "Coffee and food in fifteen minutes."

"Fine." Evie kept her head down as she walked past him and down the hallway to the guest bedroom on trembling legs. She closed the door behind her before leaning thankfully back against it, breathing out a sigh of relief at being away from all that brooding male intensity.

How was she supposed to stay here, no matter what the reason, when Ian's anger was a living, breathing vortex of emotion?

He wasn't giving her a choice, had told her she was staying here. End of subject. Well, they would see about that, but first she needed to wash away the feel and memory of being at Cezar Fescaru's uncertain mercy, even if it had been only for a few hours.

She at least felt cleaner after the shower and washing her hair, emerging from the bathroom to find a black T-shirt and gray sweats plus a black toweling robe lying on the bed. Evidence that Ian had been into the bedroom while she was in the adjoining bathroom.

Not that she imagined he'd been sent into a haze of lust at the thought of her naked in the shower. Ian's attitude toward her since this morning had been far from lover-like.

The T-shirt reached halfway down her thighs, but she didn't bother wearing the sweats after discovering they were far too big, even tied tightly about her waist and with the bottoms of the legs turned up three or four times. The robe also swamped her and reached almost down to her ankles. She had to turn the sleeves back half a dozen times before her hands became visible. But the robe was warm, and she wasn't about to join Ian in the kitchen wearing only the T-shirt.

He turned from the hob when she entered the kitchen a few minutes later, his gaze sweeping over her from her head to her bare toes before he turned back to whatever it was he was cooking. "Help yourself to juice and coffee. The omelet and toast will be ready in a few minutes."

Evie continued to watch him as she sat down gingerly on one of the chairs around a table that was already laid with cutlery and napkins for two people. There was also the promised pot of coffee, along with a jug of fresh orange juice. Evie poured some of the latter into her glass before drinking it down in one thirsty swallow. After which she filled both glasses, and then the coffee cups, before glancing back to where Ian was still working in front of the hob.

This was the second time he had cooked for her, and the half a huge stuffed omelet he turned onto a plate before placing it in front of her and then bringing over a rack of toast and some butter looked and smelled as delicious as the spaghetti Bolognese he had made the previous evening.

Ian wished he could say that his temper had cooled while Evie took a shower. Unfortunately, that wasn't the case. He had only to think of the what-ifs and what *could* have happened earlier for his rage to build to epic proportions.

He couldn't even look at Evie right now without wanting to pick her up and shake her for having behaved so recklessly, despite his warnings. She needed a lesson in how to start listening, to accept that he knew what he was talking about when it came to men like Cezar Fescaru.

It would have been better if she didn't look so much like a child playing grown up in his overlarge clothing. But ultimately it made no difference to what had to happen once they had eaten.

"Eat," he instructed tersely as he brought over his own plate with the second half of the omelet on it and sat down opposite her at the table.

"Ian—"

"I said eat," he rasped, picking up his own fork and cutting into the steaming-hot omelet.

The two of them ate in silence for several minutes before Evie attempted to speak again. "Ian, I just want—"

"For some strange reason, I really don't give a damn what you want," he taunted. "Now eat the rest of your damned omelet before it gets cold."

Evie placed her fork carefully down on the side of the plate, having eaten only half the omelet. The churning of her stomach told her she wasn't going to be able to eat any more until they had gotten this promised conversation over with. "I can't eat with you sitting there quietly fuming at me."

He eyed her coldly. "Would you rather I fumed loudly?"

"Yes." She pushed her chair back noisily as she stood up. "I know what I did was wrong. I know it could so easily have had a different outcome. But you sitting there punishing me with your silence isn't making it any better."

He gave a hard and derisive laugh. "I haven't even begun your *punishment* yet."

Evie stilled, her knuckles showing white as her hands tightly gripped the back of her chair. "What do you mean?"

Ian finished the last two bites of his omelet and took a drink of coffee before answering her. "I get that your mother died when you were young, that your father was an alcoholic, and your brother was too weak a character to take on the role as head of the family. I get all that and the reasons for it. But it's given you too big a sense of your own capabilities. The belief that you can reason or charm your way out of any situation or difficulty."

She shook her head. "That isn't true. I've never thought that."

"Yeah, you have," he confirmed wearily. "There's nothing wrong with either self-confidence or independence." He stood up to clear the plates and condiments off the table. "Until one or both of them almost gets you killed." He straightened. "So, table or chair?"

Evie blinked at this sudden and illogical change of subject. "Sorry?"

"Table or chair," he repeated grimly. "Because in a few seconds, I assure you you're going to be bent over one of them while I spank your ass for you as a physical reminder to never put your life recklessly in danger ever again."

CHAPTER 14

Evie gaped at him. "You have got to be kidding me!"

Ian met her outraged gaze unblinkingly. "Do I look as if I'm kidding?"

The grim intent in his expression told her that was the last thing he was doing. But he couldn't seriously expect her to bend over the table or a chair while he—

This was not happening. She didn't care how angry Ian was, or that he had been proven correct as to what might happen to her if she went looking for the Fescarus. She had no intention of suffering the indignity of having her ass spanked as if she were a disobedient child rather than a grown woman who had been making decisions for herself and her family for more years than she wanted to think about.

"Okay, table it is." Ian nodded. "Lift up the back of the robe and bend over the table."

"I'll do no such thing!" She took a step back, not forward.

He narrowed his eyes. "The quicker we get this out of

the way, the sooner we can move forward."

"I'm not bending over any— Ian!" Her protest came out as a surprised squeak as she suddenly found herself bent over the kitchen table with her bottom bared as Ian threw up the back of her robe and T-shirt to her waist. He'd moved so fast, Evie hadn't had chance to stop him. "Let me up this instant." Her voice shook with anger as she pushed against the table and tried to straighten. Something she failed to do with Ian's hand placed firmly in the middle of her back. "You fucking bast—" *Oh my God…*

The hard smack of Ian's hand against her bared flesh stung like the devil. Until it didn't. What came after that sting owed nothing to pain and everything to a deluge of pleasurable sensations such as Evie had never experienced before.

She— No, not her, her *body* was actually aroused by being spanked?

Heat radiated from between her thighs.

Her nether lips had become slick and open.

Her clit felt swollen.

Her nipples were hard and engorged, their stiffness rubbing against the unyielding wooden tabletop.

"Ian…?" Her gasp was breathy as he landed another smack across her bottom cheeks.

"Ten," he bit out between gritted teeth.

"Ten what?" Evie's brain was so overloaded with her physical responses to Ian spanking her that it couldn't process the meaning of his words.

"I'm going to spank you five times as punishment for almost getting yourself killed, and another five for almost getting someone else killed." His voice was a sensuous whisper close to her ear, his hand now caressing the stinging globes of her bottom. "Anything you want to say in your defense?"

Evie was sure she had plenty of things she *could* say. She just couldn't think of a single one of them when her brain had gone into sensual meltdown.

This was wrong, so very wrong, on so many levels. And yet there was no denying her aroused response.

"I'll take your silence as a no," Ian said with satisfaction as he straightened to land another stinging blow against her bared flesh.

Evie thought it was about the sixth time Ian spanked her that she heard the low groans of pleasure filling the otherwise silence of the room and realized she was the one making them. Not only that, but she was standing on tiptoe so that she could lift her bottom up in eagerness to receive every one of those smacks.

"Stretch out your arms and grasp the other side of the table," Ian instructed. "Don't move unless I tell you to."

Evie felt as if she had completely lost control of her own body as her arms moved obediently across the table, allowing her to grip tightly onto the opposite edge. This new position almost lifted her feet off the floor completely and her swollen nipples now chaffed against the hard tabletop.

"Part your legs for me. Exactly like that," Ian murmured approvingly as she instantly did as he instructed.

Ian enjoyed looking at the rapidly reddening cheeks of Evie's bottom, but this new position allowed him to see her swollen pussy lips too. Red as well as swollen, and awash with the flow of her juices.

Not that he had doubted her arousal. Those groans and the way Evie had begun to lift her bottom every time he spanked her told him this was no longer a punishment but a pleasure.

For both of them.

His cock was hard as steel inside his boxers, the head achingly sensitized, pre-cum leaking from the slit at the top. All caused from baring Evie's ass and spanking her.

Which reminded him… "Seven," he landed this smack hard against the glowing left cheek of her bottom, loving the way the flesh wobbled from the force of it. "Eight." This one landed on the right cheek, with another one of those delicious wobbles and a deepening of the flush to those edible cheeks. "More?" He deliberately held back from administering the last two as he unfastened and unzipped his jeans, pulling his boxers down and allowing his cock to spring free of its confinement. "Evie?"

"More," she encouraged, her voice somewhere between a gasp and a sob.

"Sure?"

"S-sure." She nodded her head, the darkness of her hair falling forward and preventing him from seeing her face. "Please..." she groaned achingly.

Ian slowly pumped his cock as he administered the last two spanks in rapid succession before trailing the fingers of that hand across and down those burning cheeks to stroke them along her drenched pussy. Evie groaned in response as he scooped up the juices gushing from between her swollen nether lips and rubbed it over her clit and between the hot red cheeks of her bottom.

"Oh God. *God!*" Evie groaned as she pushed back against his marauding fingers.

"Is this what you want?" Ian rubbed the slick head of his cock against her opening.

"Yes. Oh God, yes!" She lifted up, squirming against his cock as she tried to impale herself on that silken hardness, sighing her relief and pleasure as the bulbous head easily breached her well-lubricated pussy lips.

Ian gripped her hips tightly to hold her in position as

the contracting and greedy walls of her pussy tried to suck him in. "No, damn it." He gave her bottom a warning tap. "We do this my way." He began to enter her slowly, one inch at a time, stilling once his balls were snug against the heat radiating off her bottom.

The friction of flesh against flesh and the abrasive curls about the base of Ian's cock caused Evie to gasp at the mixture of pleasure and pain.

"Am I hurting you?"

"No. No, it's fine."

"Only fine?" he drawled as he once again dragged his cock over that sensitive cluster of nerves inside her.

"Better than fine," she assured him hastily in case he decided to stop.

Evie had never thought of herself like this. Never imagined she would *enjoy* having her bottom spanked. Or, with Ian standing behind her and hidden from view, living the fantasy of having this almost anonymous cock claiming her so masterfully at the same time as she knew she was completely safe.

She had never been as aroused as she was right now.

Ian held her hips steady as he slowly pulled back again, the length of his cock scraping over those nerves inside her and sending shockwaves of pleasure coursing through and over her.

Her fingers tightened on the edge of the table as he slammed back into her, once again filling her completely, before he began the torment of once again slowly withdrawing.

The pleasure was unimaginable as she felt her climax churning deep inside her, not slowly but hurtling toward her throbbing clit and the trembling walls of her pussy.

"Please," she pleaded as that cock slowly began to withdraw. "Harder!" She pushed back, needing that cock deep inside her, pleasuring her, taking her to the heights that remained just beyond her rea— "Yes!" she gasped as Ian thrust his cock back inside her before his hips began to piston, thrusting his cock faster and harder inside her and releasing a climax that was so huge and prolonged as Ian began to pump inside her that Evie felt the darkness overwhelming her.

"Evie?" Something tapped lightly against her cheek. "Evie, for God's sake wake up!"

Ian.

And he sounded worried. Overwrought, in fact.

"Jesus Christ, what have I done?" he muttered achingly.

Evie tried to push her way through the darkness, but as she felt herself being lifted into Ian's arms, she gave in to the need to snuggle against the warmth of his chest, instinctively knowing nothing could be wrong with her world if Ian was in it.

Besides, she didn't want to wake up just yet if it meant losing this connection between the two of them, much preferred to keep her eyelids closed and bask in the warmth of the afterglow of their lovemaking.

Wild and uninhibited lovemaking that had culminated in the most explosive, sweetly agonizing climax of her life.

She fell gratefully back into the darkness to dream of that lovemaking happening all over again.

It really was dark outside when Evie woke up again. The lamp on the bedside table was switched on and revealed that she was lying on the bed in the spare bedroom Ian had said was for her use. She frowned her disappointment that it wasn't Ian's bed. That frown deepened as she turned over and realized he wasn't in the bed beside her.

"He isn't here."

Not completely alone, after all, her gaze seeking out the presence of that familiar voice.

Ethan stepped forward from the shadows, that mischievous gleam in his eyes noticeably absent as he stood beside the bed looking down at her. "Ian's gone, Evie."

"Where?" She pulled herself up against the pillows, giving a wince as her well-used body protested at the movement. She turned on her side as she realized lying on her back wasn't a good idea when her bottom was stinging with discomfort. "Did something happen to Adam?"

"Your brother is fine," Ethan rasped his irritation. "It seems that by the time they reached Markovic's house, the Russian had decided that Adam really was going to work for him— On the legitimate side of his business," he hastened to assure her as Evie frowned. "He's agreed to pay Adam's debts and wipe off what he owes Utopia in exchange for Adam working for him for the next two years."

"He has?"

"I think Markovic has taken a liking to him."

"But—"

"Would you for once in your life forget about your damned brother and think of yourself?" Ethan scowled.

"Me?" she echoed blankly. "I have nothing to think about." Nothing that knowing where Ian had gone wouldn't cure, at least.

Ethan sat on the side of the bed, hazel-colored gaze full of concern. "Ian said he hurt you."

Evie's face blazed with heat at the memory of the hurt he was no doubt referring to. Who would have thought having her bottom spanked by Ian would be so erotically wild, she had actually passed out from the depth of her orgasm?

She frowned at Ethan. "He told you what happened?"

"Well…not in any detail, no." Ethan looked at her searchingly as the deepening warmth in her cheeks no doubt gave him further insight into what form that supposed *hurt* had taken. "The stupid bastard!" He stood impatiently, running an agitated hand through the dark thickness of his hair as he began to pace the bedroom. "Sweet *fucking* hell!"

"Ian left because he thought he'd hurt me?" Evie wanted clarity on that before she decided how to react to it. To her mind, there were only two possible responses to Ian having walked out of her life a second time. Because he didn't want her. Which she didn't believe. Or because the depth of their lovemaking had scared the hell out of him. Neither of which was acceptable.

"He called me." Ethan nodded. "Asked me to come and sit with you. He said he'd been brutal and that it would be better for both of you if he wasn't here when you woke up."

Evie supposed to Ian it *could* have looked as if she had passed out because— No, it couldn't, damn it. She had been with him one hundred percent in the fierceness of their lovemaking, had *begged* him to go harder. She had impaled herself on him like a cat in heat, for God's sake. How could Ian possibly have mistaken that for anything but her complete enjoyment—

Because afterward, I passed out and didn't tell him, reassure him, that I was okay.

More than okay, to be honest. It had thrilled and excited her, added to her complete abandon, that Ian was as out of control as she was.

Evie was thankful Ian had at least put the black T-shirt back on her before leaving. She swung her legs to the side of the bed and sat up, wincing slightly as it put pressure on her sore bottom, giving Ethan a challenging glare as he obviously saw that wince and raised a mocking brow. "Is Ian coming back?"

He nodded, humor once against dancing in those hazel-green eyes. "I'm supposed to call him after I've driven you home."

"Then do it."

"Now?"

"Now— No," She stood up. "Would you please take me back to my apartment first so I can shower and change, and then bring me back here? Then—and don't take this personally—I would like you to leave."

Ethan grinned. "Going to give him hell, are you?"

"You have no idea!" she stated determinedly.

"I'm guessing you would prefer he doesn't have prior knowledge of that?"

"Oh yes." If Ian thought for one moment he could walk out on her—again—without so much as saying good-bye, then he had another think coming.

This time, Evie was going to demand the truth. Because there was no way she would believe, after their off-the-charts lovemaking earlier, that Ian found their lovemaking, or her, *boring and predictable*.

Something else was going on here, and this time, she intended demanding to know what it was.

CHAPTER 15

Ian threw the keys to his car into the bowl in the hallway of his apartment.

An apartment that seemed eerily quiet.

He had lived here for five years now. Well, lived was perhaps too broad a description when it held little in the way of warmth or personal items. It was simply a place for him to crash in between assignments for Knight Security.

Even so, it had never felt *empty* before.

Nor had he felt alone here.

Or lonely.

It felt all those things now that Evie was no longer here to warm it. To warm him.

"Are you going to stand out here in the hallway all evening?"

Ian felt the color leech from his cheeks as he stared at Evie standing in the doorway to the kitchen.

Was she even real, or had he gone completely out of his mind?

She *looked* real.

She looked good enough to eat, was what she looked!

Her dark hair was a wild cascade about her shoulders. It looked even darker against the red blouse she wore tucked into low-rider black jeans. Her bare feet were taking advantage of the underfloor heating.

Surely he couldn't have dreamed up that last part?

"Well?" She quirked a challenging brow.

He swallowed before speaking. "You can't be real." He gave shake of his head.

"Like me to pinch you to prove it?" Wry amusement danced in sapphire-blue eyes.

"Ethan told me you'd left."

"I did." She shrugged. "Ethan took me back to my apartment so I could shower and change. Then he brought me back and called you before leaving again."

No, he definitely couldn't have made that up. Which meant that Evie really was still here. In his apartment. Waiting for him to come home.

Ian felt his heart squeeze painfully as he realized that for the first time, that was exactly what his apartment now felt like. That the cold loneliness had gone and it was now full of warmth and color. Because Evie was in it.

Why was she? He had hurt her earlier, humiliated her, and then she had passed out. Was that why she was still here? So that she could tell him exactly what she thought of him?

He steeled himself for that as he moistened his dry lips. "Why?"

Evie hadn't had too long to wait after Ethan left before she heard Ian enter the apartment. Then the metallic sound of his car keys being tossed into the bowl in the hallway. Followed by complete silence.

The longer that silence lasted, the more her nerves had strung out, until in the end, she hadn't been able to bear it any longer and had moved to stand in the kitchen doorway.

Ian had looked so…alone.

There was no other way for Evie to describe that pained look on his face. He looked alone and lonely. As if the walls of his apartment were closing in on him.

Until she spoke to him. The color had drained from his cheeks at the same time as a fire had flared briefly in his eyes, before dampening down again as he stared at her blankly.

She had wanted to go to him then. To put her arms about his waist and hold him tight. To reassure him he wasn't alone. That he never needed to be alone again unless he wanted to be.

Caution held her back; there was no guarantee Ian wanted any of those things. Especially from her.

She gave another shrug. "Because, for one thing, you don't get to walk away from me a second time without saying good-bye."

He gave another wince of pain before bringing his emotions back under his control. "Good-bye."

Evie smile ruefully. "And that explanation as to why you left the first time."

"That's two things."

"I'm not counting."

Neither was Ian. Not really. Evie could have a hundred questions she wanted to ask him, and he knew he owed her the answer to every single one of them. Except he knew, ultimately, it would make no difference to the outcome.

He did owe Evie an apology for his behavior earlier, however. He just didn't know where to begin doing that. He had been off his head with worry about her until he saw her again in Fescaru's office, and it had been that worry and the angry relief that followed which had fueled his behavior once they were back in his apartment.

Not good enough, Knight.

Damn it, he had stretched her facedown across the kitchen table, thrown up the robe and T-shirt before spanking her backside until it gleamed a bright and rosy red. After which he had pounded his cock into her like a fucking maniac. Possessing her, *claiming* her, when he had no right to do either.

How did he even begin to apologize for that?

"Don't even think about apologizing for our lovemaking earlier." Evie's eyes were narrowed in warning as she seemed to guess his thoughts. "Not unless you want to bring out my violent tendencies."

His frown felt pained. "I'd deserve it."

Evie drew in a deep breath, knowing this was an all-or-nothing moment. Besides what did she have to lose? "Ian, I don't know what explanation you're torturing yourself with, but as far as I'm concerned, our lovemaking earlier was exactly that. Love. Making. Because I do love you. I've always loved you. I will always love you," she added huskily.

His face paled deathly white. "No…"

"Yes," she insisted firmly. "Don't panic, I'm not asking you to love me back." The deathly pallor was unmistakable, as was his not admitting to having those same feelings for her. "I want you to know that nothing, absolutely nothing the two of us did together, could ever be anything but lovemaking to me. And I did love it, Ian," she continued determinedly. "You had to have known that. The wildness of it. The *raw* passion and desire. It was amazing."

"And then you passed out."

"With pleasure. Only with pleasure. You almost blew the top of my head off with the depth of that pleasure," she acknowledged self-derisively before sobering. "I would do it all again right now if I thought my bottom could take it."

226 | CAROLE MORTIMER

Some of the heavy weight had started to lift from Ian's chest at hearing Evie tell him she loved him, and it lifted completely as she confessed to feeling the same mind-blowing pleasure he had when he was inside her earlier. He had owned her in that moment, but she had also owned him. Completely.

He'd taken a step toward her before he even realized what he was doing, bringing himself up short once he did. "I can't," he choked. "I can't love you. Or have anyone love me. I don't— I can't—" Fucking hell, what was that dampness on his cheeks? It couldn't be tears—could it? How *fucking* humiliating was that? "It would seem that you're in love with a wuss." He scrubbed the evidence of those tears roughly from his face.

"Showing emotion isn't being a wuss." She stepped out into the hallway and grasped his arm with both hands before pulling him into the kitchen with her. "It's hiding from those emotions, denying they exist, that's being a wuss." She looked at him searchingly. "Tell me why, Ian. Why can't you love me? Love anyone? Not that it's going to make any difference, because I'll still love you anyway."

Ian gave what he could only described as a watery laugh. "That's because you have to be the most stubborn woman I've ever known."

"There is that." She chuckled briefly. "Talk to me," she

encouraged softly. "Please."

He dropped down heavily on one of the stools at the breakfast bar as his legs threatened to collapse beneath him, his gaze lowered on the marble top. "Like you, I'm a twin." Just saying those words twisted a knife inside his chest.

Evie stilled. Ian had never mentioned having any siblings, let alone a twin. Was it a brother or a sister—

"My sister's name was Sophie," he continued evenly.

Evie felt the color drain from her own cheeks. "Was…?"

Ian's eyes were filled with the depths of his private hell as he looked up at her. "She died. No, damn it," he rasped. "She didn't die, she was killed by the bastard that abducted and raped her."

Oh my God…

Evie had to lean against the breakfast bar as she swayed. "When?"

"Ten years ago." He ran his hand across his face. "I was still in the army then. I… They gave me compassionate leave so I could come home and help search for her. I arrived home just in time to be told they had found her body buried in a shallow grave in some woods not far from the hospital where she worked as a nurse. She had been there almost from the beginning." He stood up, as if sitting still was an impossibility. "They said—said she had been dead for about a week. Which meant she was killed within hours of being abducted." His face was ravaged with the grief of that loss.

This was worse, so much worse than anything Evie could ever have imagined. Adam was irresponsible and reckless, but he was her twin, and she loved him. If anything ever happened to him, she would be inconsolable with grief.

As Ian was for his twin.

"Did—" She swallowed. "Did they get whoever was responsible?"

Ian nodded. "An ex-patient who had become obsessed with her. He died in prison a year later," he added harshly.

Evie drew her breath in sharply. "Did you…?"

"Have anything to do with it?" he finished scathingly. "If I'd thought of it, I might have done. But no, it wasn't me. He apparently became obsessed with the daughter of one of the other prisoners. Stole photographs of her. Letters. The other prisoner found out and decided his daughter wasn't going to be the bastard's next victim when he got out of prison."

Evie didn't know what to say. There was nothing she could say that would ease any of Ian's pain. Any connection between siblings was close, but the one between twins was even more so. They had been in the womb together, were a part of each other even when they were apart. To have lost his twin would have been almost like losing a limb.

She moistened her lips with the tip of her tongue. "The photograph next to your bedside…"

"What about it?" Ian questioned sharply.

"Is that her? I only noticed it because there are no other photographs in the apartment." Nothing to say anyone lived here, and it was logical that the one photograph Ian did have would be of his beloved twin. "What happened to Sophie is…horrible, and you know that I understand how much worse it is as she was your twin. Adam is useless, I freely admit that, but I still love him. But I don't understand why you think you don't deserve to be loved. Why you won't allow yourself to love."

He snorted. "I should have been here, damn it. If I hadn't joined the army and been off in some godforsaken place—"

"It would have made no difference," Evie cut in softly. "Ian, Sophie was twenty-five years old. She was a nurse. Had probably lived on her own for years. Adam and I haven't lived in the same house since we were in our teens. I didn't even *know* he was missing for three days. There is no way your being in England would have made any difference to whether or not Sophie was abducted."

"You don't know that!"

"I know that for the past two days, I've been inwardly

beating myself up for being too hard on Adam the last time we met and denying him the money he asked for. The Fescarus could as easily have killed him as made him work for them. *You* were the one who helped me to see that I'm not responsible for him, that Adam is in charge of his own life. If Sophie was anything like you, then I'm guessing she was an independent young woman with a mind of her own. Your being here would have changed nothing, Ian," she repeated firmly. "People like the man you've described find a way to get what they want."

"He killed my baby sister." Ian's voice shook with emotion.

And Evie's heart ached for him. "That's right, *he* killed her, not you. Surely a therapist or psychiatrist could have told you... No?" She frowned as he shook his head.

"No." He gave a sharp shake of his head. "My cousins were great, but I couldn't talk to them either. My parents were devastated. Inconsolable. I...don't go home much anymore. Not for the past ten years."

"So your parents lost both their children instead of one?"

"What the fuck do you know about it?" His voice rose angrily, his eyes glittering darkly. "Your father was a fucking drunk who didn't know you were alive half the time, so how can you possibly relate to how it feels to look at my parents and see— Fuck! Fuck, fuck, *fuck*," he repeated with feeling. "This is why I can't be with anyone, Evie," he rasped self-disgustedly, hands clenched at his sides. "Why I walked away from you three years ago. Why I walked away from you today too. I'll hurt you, Evie. I did hurt you, damn it. I'll say or do something that will hurt you again. Until you can't bear to look at me or be around me anymore." He turned his back on her, as if looking at her hurt too much.

And that, Evie realized, was the reason Ian was afraid to love.

Because if he loved, then he also risked losing the person he loved.

Risked them one day no longer loving him.

She could try sympathizing, maybe even cajoling, but this belief was so ingrained in Ian now, she didn't think either of those things was going to get through to him. No, sympathy wasn't the way through this.

"Sophie wouldn't have wanted you to be alone like this."

"You can't know that," he growled.

"Yes, I can. I didn't know Sophie, and I'm sorry that I never will, but I know you. You're a good man, Ian. A man who deserves to be loved more than any other man I know. You *are* loved," she assured him huskily. "Whether you want to be or not. You know, Ian," she continued as he still looked unconvinced, "the last thing I ever thought you were was a coward."

"What the fuck—!" He had turned to face her, his eyes glittering with anger now. "Was I coward when I tried to protect you by sending you home from Utopia? When I came to see you the next day and then stayed with you to protect you from the Fescarus? When I walked into that fucking warehouse today surrounded by the Russian and Romanian mafia, not even knowing if you were still alive?"

"No, you weren't a coward then." Evie realized Ian believed, because he hadn't saved Sophie, that he *had* to save all the other people he could. And when he didn't, he blamed himself.

"Then how dare you call me a fucking coward?"

A slow and mocking smile began to curve her lips. "I dare because I've realized the one thing big strong *superhero* Ian Knight *is* frightened of is me."

Ian stilled, the protest dying on his lips unspoken, as he continued to stare at her for long and yet timeless minutes. "You're right," he finally acknowledged heavily. "You scare the shit out of me. You're reckless and headstrong. Stay in buildings when someone is shooting them up. Become involved with a heartless bastard like me. Fearlessly confront the heads of the mafia and *bratva*. You're going to get yourself seriously hurt or killed if you carry on the way you are."

She arched dark brows. "Then isn't that more reason for you to continue protecting me rather than walking away?"

"I did continue protecting you, damn it." He glared. "I may have walked away three years ago, but I didn't leave you high and dry. I had someone check on you every few months. Made sure you were safe."

"Why?"

"Because someone had to!" he bit out angrily.

Evie's breath caught in her throat. All this time… All those years… "Is that the only reason?"

"What other reason could there be?"

"This," she said confidently as she covered the distance between them before moving up on tiptoe and kissing him hard on the lips. "I love you, and I need you to continue protecting me. You, not some nameless, faceless man you pay to do it."

His breathing was ragged. "And who's going to protect you from me?"

"You are. And every time I do something stupid or reckless, you're going to lay me out across this table again and pound some sense into me."

"I am?"

"God, I hope so." She nodded. "That was the most erotic experience of my life. It would be a pity if it only happened the once."

Ian looked at her searchingly, able to see the conviction in the steadiness of her gaze. Able to see her love for him shining out just as unwaveringly in those clear blue eyes.

Evie *loved* him.

He had no idea why or how she did, but he couldn't doubt it when she looked at him like she was right now. As if he were the sun, the moon, and the stars to her. Her everything.

If he allowed her to leave his life again now, he would be back in that cold isolation he had felt when he walked back into his apartment earlier. Alone. Lonely. Always alone. Because Evie wasn't here.

He had spent so many years protecting his heart, believing that he didn't deserve to be loved. Evie loved him anyway.

And she was right, Sophie wouldn't have wanted him to live his life without love in it. Without loving or being loved in return.

Evie had opened up her heart to him just now. She deserved that he do the same to her.

He held out his hand, palm up. "Will you come with me?"

She didn't even hesitate to place her hand in his. "Always."

His heart was beating double time as his fingers curled about hers, and he turned to lead the way out of the kitchen, down the hallway, and into his bedroom.

"Why, Mr. Knight, what are your intentions?" she teased.

Ian turned to face her and took both her hands in his as they stood beside the bed. "You showed me your heart. Now I'm going to show you mine."

The teasing left her eyes as she looked into his face searchingly. "You are?"

"Mm. You asked why I walked away three years ago. Why I walked away again today. *This* is why, Evie." He released her hand to turn and pick up the photograph from the bedside cabinet before handing it to her.

She stared down at the image for so long, Ian was sure his heart had stopped beating altogether. He certainly wasn't breathing. The combination was making him feel light-headed.

Then he saw the tears on Evie cheeks, and he was certain his heart had stopped beating.

She drew in a deep and shaky breath as she looked up at him. "It's me."

"Yes."

"You took it three years ago. When we packed a picnic and spent the day beside the river?"

"Yes."

"Has it been here ever since?"

"Yes."

"You loved me then."

"Yes."

"You love me now."

"Yes."

"You stupid *bastard*!" She placed the photograph back on the bedside table before pummeling his chest with her fists, her face flushed with temper. "You stupid, stupid *bastard*." The tears flowed unchecked down her cheeks. "God, Ian, you are so— I could—" She collapsed into his waiting arms, her own arms clinging about his waist. "How could you do that to us? How could you love me three years ago and still walk away?"

"I thought I had to."

Her eyes were awash with those tears when she raised her head and looked at him. "Let's have an agreement in future, shall we? You are so terrible at it, I'll do the thinking for both of us."

All Ian heard was the word "future."

For the first time in a very long time, he was starting to believe he might have one.

His reasons for walking away from her three years ago, for denying his feelings for her, now seemed…obsolete.

In the matter of a few minutes, Evie had made them
so. Not by belittling his reasons, but by acknowledging
them, understanding them, talking about them, and then
dismissing them.

He should have told her all this sooner. Should have
explained his fears. They had wasted *three years*. Three
fucking years. How could he have been so…so… Evie, was
right. He was stupid. *Had been* stupid. But that stopped
right here and now. He didn't care how selfish it was. He
wanted Evie, and he wasn't going to let her go this time.

His arms tightened about her waist. "I love you, Evie.
I love you so much," he repeated emotionally. "I never want
to be without you again. These past three years have been…
God, I don't even want to think about it!" He shuddered at
the memory of the loneliness of being without the woman
he loved. "Can you ever forgive me?"

She blinked back the tears as she touched his cheek
gently. "I already have."

"Then marry me," he urged. "For God's sake, for *my*
sake, marry me and put me out of my misery."

"Yes." Evie didn't even need to think about it. Not for a
second.

This was the man she loved. The man she had always
loved. The man she would always love.

The man who she now had no doubt loved her as

completely as she loved him.

Their twins, conceived on the night Ian spanked Evie, were born prematurely eight months later, as confirmation that Ian could indeed still *reproduce* following Evie's attempt to castrate him.

"Sophie Jane looks just like you, Mrs. Knight." Ian held the miracle of his newly born daughter tenderly in his arms, tears glistening in his eyes and spilling over as he looked down at their beautiful daughter.

"And Simon Ethan looks just like you, Mr. Knight." Evie could feel the tears falling down her own cheeks as she cuddled their son.

Tears of happiness.

A happiness and love that grew deeper and stronger every day.

Ian came to sit on the side of the bed where Evie lay resting following several hours of childbirth. "My parents are going to want to come in and see you all in a few minutes. But before they do I want to tell you again how much I love you, Evie, and how thankful I am that you love me."

Evie reached up to kiss him. "Always."

For news on upcoming releases please sign up to my mailing list/newsletter: http://www.eepurl.com/2rfzz

Facebook: http://www.facebook.com/CaroleMortimerAuthor

Twitter: http://twitter.com/@carole_mortimer

Visit my website: www.carolemortimer.co.uk

Or email me at: contact@carolemortimer.co.uk

If you have enjoyed reading Enticing Ian, please don't forget to leave a review of this book.

ABOUT THE AUTHOR

Carole Mortimer is the author of over 220 novels, contemporary and Regency romance. She is a USA Today Bestselling Author. Recipient of the 2015 RWA Lifetime Achievement Award. Received the 2014 Pioneer for Romance Romantic Times Award. Entertainment Weekly Top 10 Author. She was also recognized by Queen Elizabeth II in 2012 for her 'outstanding service to literature'.

She is happily married to Peter. They have 6 sons, and live on the beautiful Isle of Man. She also loves to hear from Readers!

Other Books By Carole Mortimer

Knight Security Series: spin-off to Alpha Series:
Resisting Alexandre (Knight Security 0.5)
Defying Asher (Knight Security 1)
Challenging Gabriel (Knight Security 2)
Capturing Caleb (Knight Security 3)
Tempting Zander (Knight Security 4)
Enticing Ian (Knight Security 5)
Seducing Ethan (Knight Security 6)

ALPHA series:
Christmas Alpha (Alpha 1)
Dark Alpha (Alpha 2)
Shadow Alpha (Alpha 3)
Midnight Alpha (Alpha 4)
Renegade Alpha (Alpha 5)
Warrior Alpha (Alpha 6)
Rogue Alpha (Alpha 7)
Savage Alpha (Alpha 8)
Series now complete.

Regency Unlaced Series:
The Duke's Mistress (Regency Unlaced 1)
Claimed by the Marquis (Regency Unlaced 2)

Taken by the Earl (Regency Unlaced 3)
Pursued by the Marquis (Regency Unlaced 4)
Desired by a Lord (Regency Unlaced 5)
Captured by a Gentleman (Regency Unlaced 6)
Pleasured by a Duke (Regency Unlaced 7)
Seduced by a Marquis (Regency Unlaced 8)
Tamed by the Earl (Regency Unlaced 9)
This series is now complete.

Regency Sinners Series:
Wicked Torment (Regency Sinners 1)
Wicked Surrender (Regency Sinners 2)

48301384R00152

Made in the USA
San Bernardino, CA
22 April 2017